## ESCAPE FROM DEATH

Paul Towers was scuba diving for abalone when he had his first narrow escape from death. Only luck and his wife Sybil saved him from drowning. Other "accidents" followed, sinister and inexplicable. Paul's life in Orchestra Beach had always been smooth and secure, almost stodgily conservative for such a young man. His marriage of three years was happy. His self-made success as the publisher of the local weekly made him a candidate for every local betterment committee. Now, behind the mask of devoted husband and admired civic leader, he had to play the double role of hunter and hunted. The pleasant California town suddenly became a place of irrational horrors.

Here is a cliff-hanging tale of a cleverly concealed struggle for the country's safety, and of a man, fighting for survival, whose life would be forfeited if he told the truth.

# THE DEATH OF ME YET

## BY WHIT MASTERSON

PINNACLE BOOKS • NEW YORK CITY

THE DEATH OF ME YET

A Pinnacle Books edition, published by special arrangement with Dodd, Mead & Company.

ISBN: 0-523-00636-5

First printing, May 1975

Printed in the United States of America

PINNACLE BOOKS, INC.
275 Madison Avenue
New York, N.Y. 10016

To Johnny and Edna

# CONTENTS

# EDDIE

As he stepped off the bus, Eddie noted that the hands of the grandfather clock in the window of Klein's Jewelry stood at five fifty-nine. One minute early; yet even as he formed the thought, the big hand moved to invalidate it. The bus picked him up at eight each morning and delivered him to the plant at eight twenty-five. Each evening it returned him to this corner at six o'clock. Eddie doubted if any bus company in the United States maintained a more meticulous schedule.

The July sun, still several degrees above the horizon, burned into the back of his neck and the lifeless air draped about him like a soggy blanket. He ducked into the comparative coolness of the drugstore and paused under the rotating overhead fan as he tried to recall what Alice had told him to get. His fingers found the folded scrap of paper in his pocket which she, anticipating his forgetfulness, had placed there. *Carton Luckies, Gillette blades, tube Colgate t/paste, small Kleenex . . .*

The cashier rang up his purchases and returned eleven cents in change. "Hot enough for you, Mr. Young?"

"A real scorcher," Eddie agreed. "Of course, it's not the heat, it's the humidity." He left a dime on the counter. "I'll grab a paper on the way out."

He used the penny to weigh himself. One hundred seventy-three, about average for a man of twenty-three who stood a shade under six feet. The mirror reflected a rather average face also, neither handsome nor ugly. The coarse brown hair, clipped short, was the same shade as the wide-set eyes but lighter than the brows which separated them. The high forehead and the straight thin nose imparted an ascetic quality, that of a monk or scholar, but this was contradicted by the mouth whose corners curved naturally into a smile.

He scanned the headlines as he walked. GOLDWATER BLASTS LBJ RECORD. RIOTING RAGES IN BROOKLYN. DE GAULLE BELITTLES U.S. ROLE IN EUROPE. ATTORNEYS CLASH AT HOFFA TRIAL. The world was in its customary turmoil this final week of July, 1964. Eddie turned to the sports section. The Phillies and the Yankees continued to lead their respective leagues by narrow margins; Koufax had won his eleventh game of the season. He refolded the newspaper to its original shape. Tonight he'd be able to read the paper leisurely, now that his classes had ended and he was no longer on the dash-in-grab-a-bite-dash-out-again-to-school routine. He hoped that Alice hadn't made plans for the evening. It would be nice to stay home for a change.

"Home" was a three-story apartment building, distinguishable only by its number from the other brick and concrete units which lined Maple Street. The apartments also were virtually identical, consisting of four rooms— living room, kitchenette, bedroom and bath—although their décor differed with the taste of their occupants. Alice, along with most of the women, complained that it was too cold in the winter and too hot in the summer. Eddie, while admitting the drawbacks, was content with the apartment since it was the first home that had ever been truly his.

An episode of *I Love Lucy* was blaring from the television ("You not gonna get inta da act thees time an' thassa order!" "Why, Ricky, the idea never even entered my mind!" Laughter.) but Alice was not watching. Eddie turned it off. "Hi, hon—I'm home." She responded to the greeting without leaving the stove. Eddie lifted the brown ponytail to kiss the nape of her neck. Alice was often described as "nice-looking," that is to say, she was attractive without being beautiful. Her body, small-breasted and narrow-hipped, was almost boyish but her long graceful legs were definitely female. Tonight, as usual, she wore clothing to enhance her good points, brief white shorts and a loose blouse. Her feet, tiny for her height, were bare.

"What's for dinner?" He answered his own question. "Monday. Leftovers, naturally."

"Steak," she contradicted. "And French fries."

"You're kidding! What's the occasion?"

She gave him an odd look. "Didn't you see the mail when you came in? I left it on the table."

She followed him and stood watching while he skimmed the typewritten letter. *Edward T. Young . . . is hereby directed to report for induction . . .* When he raised his head, her lips formed the word "When?"

"Eight a.m. Tuesday. That's tomorrow." He chuckled mirthlessly. "God, they don't give a guy much advance notice, do they?"

Alice turned away suddenly, mumbling, "I'm letting your dinner burn." He pursued and placed a comforting arm about her waist. "I know, hon. It's rough. But it's not as if we have a choice."

She nodded but didn't look at him and he realized that

3

she was crying. "Hushabye, baby," he soothed, the nonsense phrase they used to express intimacy and affection; every marriage has its equivalent.

"It's just that I'm going to miss you so terribly."

"I'll bet you tell that to all your husbands," he said lightly.

"Don't joke, Eddie—please. It's been a wonderful year, hasn't it?"

"The best. Better than I could have imagined. So let's not spoil it now, okay?"

"Okay." She brushed at her eyes with the back of her hand. "You dish up the salad while I get the steaks out. No sense ruining this perfectly marvelous banquet. It's the last home-cooked meal you're going to get in a while." She forced a smile. "That's meant to cheer you up, sweetie."

Their conversation at dinner was lighthearted in tone and trivial in content, with no silences permitted, lest their thoughts turn inward. Yet the letter remained on the table between them, studiously ignored but as ominous as a ticking time bomb. While their second cup of coffee cooled, Eddie directed their attention to it again. "I've got a little packing to do."

"I'll do it for you," Alice said quickly.

"You needn't bother, hon. All they allow me to bring are a few toilet articles and a change of underwear." But he saw that she desired to perform this final wifely act, so he capitulated. "I guess I could use a shirt ironed, too. While you're doing that, mind if I dash over to Bob's for a minute? He doesn't know I'm leaving and I want to tell him good-by."

"Must you? I was looking forward to having the whole evening together." She conquered her disappointment. "All right, run along. I'd better start getting used to not having you around."

4

Bob Barnes lived within walking distance but in a section which Eddie and his neighbors referred to as "the other side of the tracks," by which they meant that the area was noticeably more affluent than their own. There were no tracks to set it apart, but a small park served the same function. The apartment buildings here were less functional in design, the décor less austere. Attractiveness rather than economy had dictated the architecture. The individual units were larger also; most were air-conditioned and some had private terraces. Their occupants were management, not labor: city officials, executives from the plant where Eddie and a large percentage of the community were employed, and professors from the university where he attended night classes. Bob Barnes was a member of the latter group.

He was working on a painting when Eddie arrived. "Christ, no, you're not interrupting anything," he said cordially. "Just dabbling. Come on in." Barnes was a handsome man of thirty-five; even in paint-streaked T-shirt and dungarees he managed to appear dashing. His lithe body was that of an athlete, his lean face with its jet-black hair and piercing blue eyes that of a cavalier. To these physical assets, he added a magnetism that Eddie found irresistible. He had never encountered anyone, man or woman, with more warmth and wit. During the past year their relationship had ripened from that of instructor and pupil to that of equals.

Barnes' easel was set up in the middle of the living room. Since he was a bachelor, there was no necessity to bow to any feminine demand for neatness. His apartment was cluttered with books, records and bric-a-brac, yet imparted the same casual charm as its occupant. There was always brandy on the table and music on the stereo; tonight it was Bach.

Eddie examined the unfinished canvas, a street scene done in the style of the French impressionists. "That's going to be great. New York?"

Barnes grinned. "The Bronx, East 173rd Street. I used to live right there, on the second floor. If I close my eyes, I can still smell it. Clear off the couch and sit down. I'll get you a drink."

"I can't stay long, Bob. I just came over to say good-by. My induction notice arrived today and I'm shoving off in the morning."

"Yeah, I know." Noting Eddie's surprise, he explained, "Hell, I have connections, my boy. I hear these things. I knew last week that you were slated to go."

"Why didn't you tip me off?"

"And spoil your weekend? Or am I mistaken, and you're just dying to get into the service?"

"I do hate to leave here," Eddie said slowly. "But since I have to, I'm kind of looking forward to it."

"The age-old male conflict between security and adventure," Barnes agreed, bringing him the brandy. "How is Alice taking it? These things are usually more traumatic for the women."

"I guess she's going to miss me."

"As a matter of fact, I'm going to miss you myself. It's been a pleasure to have you in my class, Eddie—and that's not simply a going away compliment. Most of my pupils sit there and accept what they're told. They never question, never dig beneath the surface. You're that rare animal, an intelligent man." He swirled the liqueur thoughtfully. "I hope you're not too intelligent."

"Would that be bad?"

"The world can be a horrifying place for the truly intelligent because the world is not ruled by intelligence.

You might compare it to an asylum where everyone is crazy except you—and a very few others like you."

"But if you're truly intelligent, you should be able to find a way out."

"There's no way out," Barnes said positively. "The only recourse is to run the asylum. That way you can feel that you're not actually an inmate. The sum total of my knowledge, Eddie, and I commend it to you."

Eddie set aside his brandy and stood up. "I really have to run. I wonder if I can ask a favor, Bob. Would you mind looking in on Alice now and then, to see that she's getting along all right?"

"Glad to. But I can't guarantee how long I'll be around. I wouldn't be surprised if I get my own notice before long."

Startled, Eddie said, "I thought you were exempt. I mean, after all, you've put in your service and with your job—"

"Thanks for not mentioning my age, too," Barnes said, grinning. "I'm still in the active reserve. And the rumors I hear . . . Unlike you, I wouldn't regret leaving here in the slightest. The ivory tower gets a mite confining after a while."

"Hey, wouldn't it be great if we wound up in the same place?"

"Great—but not very likely. Although you never can tell." He gave Eddie's shoulder an affectionate parting squeeze. "In the meantime, remember my advice about the asylum."

Eddie was on the corner at eight o'clock the next morning when the bus came by. It swung in toward the curb to pick him up as usual, but he waved it on. The driver looked surprised, then noted the duffel bag he carried and gave him the thumbs-up sign. The vehicle lumbered away, shy one passenger. That made the break final; otherwise, it could have seemed a routine Tuesday.

Alice had prepared a normal breakfast and her good-by had been restrained. They agreed she should not accompany him downstairs. Her face was pale but her eyes dry (although Eddie had heard her crying during the night) and he was grateful for her composure. As he gazed about at the familiar shabby yet somehow lovely store fronts—Acme Dry Cleaners, Fran's Fashions, Cork 'n' Bottle, Klein's, Rexall—he was close to tears himself.

An olive drab station wagon with an official license turned the corner and glided to a stop beside him. The uniformed driver consulted his clipboard. "Young?"

Eddie nodded, took a last look at the grandfather clock —it was four minutes past eight—and got into the automobile. He joined three other men, carrying bags similar to his own. They greeted him with the boisterous camaraderie that masks tension: "So they got you too, huh? . . . Man, they must be scraping the bottom of the barrel. . . . You'll be sor-ry! . . ."

The jocularity continued as they passed and bid farewell to familiar landmarks, then subsided as the station wagon reached the outskirts of the town and entered the rolling countryside. One of the men—Charley Somebody— attempted to strike up a conversation with the driver, who replied in curt monosyllables. Charley finally surrendered and silence reigned, each passenger occupied with his own thoughts and apprehensions.

They approached a wooded area and came upon a gate set across the road with a tall chain-link fence stretching off on either side. Two soldiers manned a guard booth that bore a sign Authorized Personnel Only—Stop for Inspection.

One of the soldiers accepted the clipboard, studied the passengers briefly and waved the vehicle through. As the gate closed behind them, Charley said loudly, "Hey, stop the car! I just remembered—it's my bowling night!" The others grinned weakly; the driver, as if fearing he were serious, trod hard on the accelerator.

Charley shrugged. "Well, I tried. Anybody got a butt?"

Eddie took a pack of Luckies from his shirt pocket and tossed it to him.

"Thanks, pal," said Charley. "How about a match?"

One of the others supplied them, asking politely, "And how are you fixed for lungs?"

Eddie did not join in the laugh. Withdrawing the cigarettes, his fingers had encountered a folded scrap of paper. He opened it and read Alice's familiar handwriting. *My name is really Irina and I love you.*

"What've you got there?" Charley asked, curious at his expression.

"Nothing," Eddie said. "Just an old grocery list." He rolled the paper into a ball and flicked it out the window. Arcing, it struck the sign that stood beside the highway. His eyes, following the flight of the tiny projectile, were caught by the Cyrillic letters and for a moment could not read them, so thorough had been his indoctrination. Then memory translated: Moscow 200 kilometers.

# PAUL

The telephone rang.

"Don't answer the damn thing," Paul whispered, "and it'll go away."

"It may be something important," Sibby argued. She rolled over and groped for the instrument. He slapped her bare rump as punishment. Her "hello" ended in an involuntary squeal and she mouthed "Darn you!" She said into the receiver, "Yes, just a minute," and handed it to him. "Ha, ha—it's for you. A man."

Paul didn't recognize the voice. "Mr. Paul Towers of 319 Cabrillo Court?"

"Speaking."

"Congratulations, Mr. Towers! Your name has been selected from among the homeowners in Orchestra Beach and, if qualified, you will be eligible to receive a free gift worth several hundred dollars."

"Okay, what are you selling?" Paul asked wearily.

"We're not *selling* anything, Mr. Towers," the other man reproved. "All we ask is a few moments of your time to assist us with a survey which our company is conducting in your area."

"Forget it. We take more magazines now than we can possibly read, we have two sets of encyclopedias and we don't need a water softener, a patio or air conditioning." He slammed down the receiver. "What a hell of a time to get hustled by a pitchman!"

Sibby chuckled. "He couldn't know you were wallowing in sin, darling. After all, it's the middle of the afternoon and most men in Orchestra Beach are busy making money, not love."

"I became my own boss so I could make what I want when I want it. In the second place, we are married. And to each other."

"Oh, I know—but I like to pretend we're not. That I'm doing something my Scotch Presbyterian conscience wouldn't let me get away with if it wasn't actually quite moral and legal. Larry says everyone has ways of compensating for his repressions."

"Hey, how did that quack get into bed with us? And when did it become Larry, by the way—instead of Dr. Shevlin?"

"We decided that first names would put us more at ease and improve communication," Sibby explained, a shade defensively. "We're meeting in each other's homes for the same reason—remember, I had the group here last week— to get away from the structured classroom environment. Larry believes that women respond better in domestic surroundings because that's where we spend most of our lives. Women are different from men, he says."

"How perceptive of Larry."

"I wish you wouldn't ridicule him. He's really a very interesting person. I'm dying for you to meet him. I've told him all about you."

"Everything?"

She giggled. "Well, not quite everything. Though you'd be surprised at some of the gals. I guess I'm easily shocked. But I still believe that there are a few matters that should be private."

"Why don't you write up all the dirt and I'll run it in the paper? Should be a great circulation booster."

She looked shocked, which was what he had intended. Sibby, together with several of her friends and other non-working wives, had enrolled in a summer class at the Institute for the Study of the Behavioral Sciences. Most of IBS's work was in the field of personnel testing, training and analysis; its clients were the university and the scientific-and-technical complex which had grown up during the past five years on the mesa behind the town. IBS had pioneered the concept of the "executive decision" games now popular in both industry and government circles. However, it also offered courses for the interested (and affluent) layman with such titles as Personal Potential, Human Interaction, Group Dynamics and Sensitivity Training. These, according to the brochure, afforded "the healthy, well-functioning adult an opportunity to identify and assess his personality resources and capacities, and to relate these to personal values and goals in an effort to develop and actualize human potential." Sibby was enjoying the experience hugely. Paul viewed it with skepticism and had resisted her efforts to involve him.

She mistook his teasing for disapproval. "You think I'm wasting my time, don't you?"

"Nope. Sure, I got to admit that I don't dig the you-tell-me-your-hangups-and-I'll-tell-you-mine bit. I'll keep my personality personal, thanks. But if it turns you on, that's fine with me."

"Well, it makes me feel like I'm doing something." She

hesitated. "Of course, if I had a baby to keep me busy . . ."

Paul groaned. "Let's not get onto that subject at a time like this."

"I think it's a very appropriate subject for a time like this. Why don't we, Paul? We've been married for over three years. People are starting to wonder about us."

"Name one."

"I'll name two. Mom and Dad. Can you blame them? When they look at us and then at Hank and Marilyn—"

"Your brother is a dozen years older than you are. And Marilyn is the original earth mother. We couldn't match them even if we tried."

"Especially if we never start. You aren't afraid of having children, are you, Paul? I hear that some men are."

"More gospel according to Shevlin? He should talk—he's a bachelor. Now there's a real coward." He got no answering smile so he said, more seriously, "You know my reasons for waiting. I want us to be on a firm financial footing before we begin our family. I've got it all planned, Sibby. Another year, maybe even less—"

"You've always got everything all planned," she grumbled. "Why can't you be madly impetuous, just once?"

"Go on," he said with a sigh. "I program myself like a computer. I decide exactly what I want my life to be—and my wife to be—and then I methodically search until I find it. And her. Anything that doesn't fit the programing is automatically rejected. Is that what you were about to say, dear?"

Sibby grinned unwillingly. "You rat. Must you remember everything I tell you in moments of anger?"

"Us computers never forget."

She raised on one elbow to study his face. "I'm a beast to complain when you give me so much happiness. It's just that, well, sometimes I'd like to believe that I didn't really fit in with your plans at all and that you married me because you couldn't help yourself."

"Okay, the truth is that I intended to marry a blonde with an IQ of 40 and a bust to match, not a smart scrawny redhead. That make you feel better?"

"Scrawny! I'll have you know I'm a perfect size seven." She added in the interest of honesty, "I suppose you could call me a bit flat-chested, though. Would you like it better if there were more of me?"

Against her mouth, he said, "I married the prettiest little broad in the prettiest little town in the world. Call it good planning if you wish. I call it good luck."

Sibby sighed happily. "I never thought I'd find a man who loves Orchestra Beach the way I do. I don't know how I'd stand it if you wanted to live somewhere else. The folks were afraid you might. They warned me you were a drifter. That's pretty funny now. They're the ones who are traveling all over the world—and I can't get you out of our backyard. I do believe your roots go even deeper than mine, and I was born here."

"I didn't have much to say about where I was born. But I intend to die right here in Orchestra Beach. And preferably in bed."

Her hands stole under his arms to fasten on his shoulders. "Not in the next fifteen minutes, I hope."

People did die in Orchestra Beach, as indeed they do everywhere, but few of the inhabitants took the possibility seriously. The community's slogan was "Heaven on Earth"; if you believed it, as most did, then immortality seemed eminently feasible. The climate helped to foster the illusion. The temperature varied only fifteen degrees from summer to winter ("The World's Shortest Thermometer"). Flowers bloomed year round and, with little to emphasize the change of seasons, time slipped by unnoticed. Furthermore, in this summer of 1970, the town itself was only sixty-five years old. Thus, if the actuarial tables are accurate, it was entirely possible that the first baby born in Orchestra Beach was still alive and vigorous.

Orchestra Beach itself was a child of the California land rush of the early 1900's, one among scores of brave new communities staked out on the sagebrush hills and crumbling bluffs above the Pacific. Most died young or, forlorn orphans, were adopted and absorbed by the burgeoning cities. In the bust that followed the boom, Orchestra Beach managed to retain its identity through geography rather than any inherent uniqueness. Midway between Los Angeles and San Diego, it was a convenient place for travelers to refuel and refresh, while its remoteness prevented its larger neighbors from gobbling it up. The founders had envisioned a spa, a western Newport, but the dream never materialized. (The rather bizarre name stemmed from a promotional scheme of the period when a pier was built and band concerts held upon it; the pier was torn down a decade later for its lumber, and few of the present residents were aware that it ever existed.) The early dreamers lost their shirts and those who fashioned other dreams during the next few years usually met the same fate. Choice beachfront acreage was sold for little and repossessed for less and those who held onto it were considered a bit mad. Orchestra Beach? Never amount to a damn thing!

It took a half-century to prove the scoffers wrong. During the twenties, Orchestra Beach was a bathing suit community, crowded in July and August, a ghost town the other ten months of the year. The depression wrought a subtle change, almost unnoticed at first. Artists and writers, seeking a refuge where creativity could flourish on scant cash, began to move in; beards and bare feet became commonplace there long before the rest of the world ever heard of hippies. They referred to Orchestra Beach as "the village"—a title now resolutely defended—and word spread that it was quaint. Money followed art as those wealthy enough to afford a second home found it a pleasant escape from urban life. The hills behind the village became dotted with homes, expensive and avant garde in design. Behind the rich came the well-to-do. Less insular than their predecessors, they demanded an active social life, so a country club was formed and a golf course laid out. Churches were organized to save their souls and schools erected to educate their children. When the freeway made commuting practical, Orchestra Beach's problem became not how to promote its growth, but how to control it.

The population explosion could not be denied. In the middle sixties the complexion of Orchestra Beach commenced to change once more. The University of California established a branch campus on the mesa, with initial emphasis on the sciences. This in turn attracted light industry, geared to space and electronics and atomics. Brisk young executives with briefcases and crew cuts replaced the artists with palettes and bare feet. Ph.D.'s were common, among them two Nobel Prize winners—and when you were introduced to a Dr. Smith, you couldn't be sure whether he could cure a rash or blow up the world. The typical citizen was under forty but above the national median in intelligence as well as income, had resided in Orchestra Beach less than ten years and considered it "a great place to live."

Paul and Sybil Towers fit the pattern in most particulars, although Sibby departed from it by being a native.

Harry Rideout Keller, her grandfather, was one of the pioneer developers. Like most, he died broke but had bequeathed his son considerable acreage that later proved more valuable than diamonds. Wilson Keller's flair was merchandising. On his worthless legacy, he built a department store, a pharmacy, a market and a hotel—all of which he eventually sold to national chains at a huge profit—plus a gaggle of smaller enterprises. He retired a wealthy man. Unlike most who make it on their own, he did not deprive his children of the opportunity to do the same. A little struggling never hurt anyone, he told them. It hadn't hurt Hank, the eldest. An engineer by education and an inventor by nature, he founded his own firm in a rented garage; Keller Corp was now one of the largest companies on the mesa. Nor had it hurt Sybil, the youngest. (A middle child, Wilson Junior, had died before any conclusion could be reached.) Sibby, who possessed a good voice, planned to pursue a career in music, an ambition her parents thoroughly approved. Instead, she married Paul Towers—which her parents did not approve at all.

It was hard to blame them. A native of Nebraska, Paul arrived in town with nothing to recommend him except an engaging grin and promptly began to court the daughter of the community's leading family. Four months later, he married her. To everyone's surprise, he did not go to work for his father-in-law but took a job selling advertising on commission for the local newspaper, an undistinguished weekly. Sure, said the cynics, but Towers knows that Will Keller won't let his daughter starve; just wait. They waited in vain. The newlyweds scrimped but survived, and when the publisher died suddenly and the *Dispatch* was up for grabs, Paul grabbed. He borrowed money—again not from Wilson Keller but from the bank—and bought the newspaper. More guts than brains, said the cynics, reversing their earlier judgment. But Paul saw that the chauvinistic town, fiercely proud of its identity, needed its own newspaper . . . if that newspaper were a good one. He set out to make it so. More businessman than journalist, he brought the comatose *Dispatch* from the handset past to the offset present, wooed the large accounts who heretofore had advertised exclusively in the Los Angeles dailies, boosted circulation with lively reporting, gimmicks and giveaways. As Orchestra Beach's appreciation of the *Dispatch* increased, so did its appreciation of its owner. Gradually he ceased to be known as Will Keller's son-in-law and became a person in his own right, an automatic candidate for every civic betterment committee and a welcome addition to any group, from Kiwanis to the Beach & Tennis Club. Those who remembered their earlier disparagement now acknowledged that Sibby had known what she was doing, after all—and none more than her own family.

"Yep, I said he was a fortune hunter," Wilson Keller admitted sheepishly. "And I was right. But it's his own fortune he's hunting, not mine. There's no stopping that boy."

To which Sibby, who did not understand her husband completely while loving him wholly, proudly agreed. And so to Mr. and Mrs. Paul Towers in the summer of 1970, today was bright and tomorrow brighter still.

The final meeting of the Fiesta committee chairmen adjourned at five minutes past two. George Dickman caught up with Paul as he left the banquet room. "Migawd!" he muttered. "I thought the damn thing would never end."

"What are you bitching about? You were asleep half the time."

"Was it obvious?" George yawned. "That silly ass Osborn, going over every last little detail, stuff we settled weeks ago—as if his precious Fiesta won't practically run itself, anyway, the same as every year."

"Your trouble is that there are only two things that interest you, sex and money."

"My trouble is that I don't get enough of either." He was one of Paul's best friends, somewhat surprising since he had been the leading suitor for Sibby's hand prior to Paul's arrival on the scene. However, he had found plenty of other girls to console him, none permanently, and the role of swinging bachelor suited him well. More so, at least on the surface, than his role as assistant manager of the Orchestra Beach First National. George Dickman belonged to the new breed of bankers and attracted more customers with his gregarious charm than he offended with his irreverent humor. "Speaking of sex," he went on, "where the hell is that abalone you've been promising me for the last year? I'm throwing an intimate little supper at my place tomorrow night and I want to dazzle the suppee with my gourmet cooking. How about it?"

"Matter of fact, Sibby and I are going out this evening after work. I'll see what I can do. Or you're welcome to come along and pry 'em up yourself if you'd like."

"Skin diving's not my bag. I believe that if God had intended man to breathe compressed air, He wouldn't have invented smog."

They stepped out of the hotel and stood for a moment on the sidewalk, blinking in the afternoon sunlight. Workmen were busy hanging canvas streamers above Coast Highway, gaudily proclaiming Orchestra Beach Fiesta Daze July 16–31.

"If it's the last thing I ever do," George said grimly, "I mean to get rid of that ghastly pun. Fiesta Daze! Jesus, that went out with sex-sational and laff riot! But then I wonder if the whole frigging Fiesta hasn't outlived its use-fulness."

Paul wondered the same thing. However, the Orchestra Beach Fiesta was a tradition, and traditions die hard. The Fiesta was a depression baby, conceived to attract tourists to a town which depended upon them for survival. Given Orchestra Beach's present complexion, it was questionable whether the benefits were worth the expense. Costs had soared astronomically as the modest three-day carnival expanded over the decades to a two-week extravaganza which included a parade with ever more elaborate floats, a fishing derby, powerboat regatta, rough water swim, a pageant which reenacted the community's founding (largely fictional), a midway for the children and a Mexican folk ballet for their parents. Yet to suggest abandoning it was a heresy stoutly resisted by the older generation who claimed it was good public relations, and to a lesser degree by the younger who relished the Mardi Gras atmosphere and the opportunity to compete in the beauty pageant and the whiskerino contest. Paul was this year's publicity chairman, a logical choice since the *Dispatch* served as the official program. The extra work was redeemed by the extra advertising revenue . . . and so Paul kept his reservations to himself.

"Of course," George continued, "I might feel different about the Fiesta if they were peddling statues of me on every street corner."

Paul laughed. "Eat your heart out." He had been persuaded, somewhat reluctantly, to pose for the figure of Tihoya, the Indian warrior who—as legend and press agentry would have it—had been Orchestra Beach's first resident. The sculptor argued that Paul's muscular body and lean aquiline features fit the popular conception of the Noble Savage ("except for the mustache") and, besides, didn't he want to help out the Fiesta? The foot-high statuettes, mass-produced in cast iron painted to resemble bronze, were a popular souvenir item, and Paul had long since learned to take the kidding with good grace. "You bought yours yet, George?"

"Damn right. I keep it in the bathroom—for inspiration. Which reminds me that I'm pissed off at you. How come you didn't tell your old buddy that the paper is up for sale?"

"Because it isn't, that's how come."

"Honest? The guy who was in to see me last Friday sure gave me the impression that it was. Credit investigator. Asked a lot of questions about the *Dispatch*, its financial position, assets and liabilities, the stuff a prospective buyer always wants to know."

"Nobody's approached me," Paul said, puzzled. "Did he tell you who he was representing?"

"I gave him the opportunity and he passed. My guess was that it's one of the newspaper chains—maybe that outfit over in Orange County—that's got eyes for expanding their empire. The *Dispatch* is an attractive property with growth potential. You should be able to get a damn good price."

"No, thanks. I'm too young to retire."

"A new owner would probably want to keep you on to run it, anyhow. At least, the fellow pumped me pretty good about the present management. How long you've owned the newspaper, your credit rating, approximate worth, standing in the community, and so on." George grinned. "I was tempted to tell him you're the biggest deadbeat ever to come out of Nebraska."

"You don't remember the investigator's name, do you?"

"No. He was an L.A. fellow, nobody I ever saw before. He gave me his card, though. I may still have it in my desk. But if you're really not interested in selling—"

"I'm not. But it never hurts to know who's interested in buying."

The Orchestra Beach business district was eight blocks long, stretching from the bed of the Padre River (which had never carried water within memory) on the north to the San Felipe estuary on the south. The Pacific Ocean acted as the western boundary; ten blocks inland, the steeply rising hills performed the same function to the east. Commercialism had spread outward from this enclave for several miles north and south along Coast Highway, but "downtown" still meant the eighty square blocks platted by the original subdividers. Zoning was stringently enforced to preserve the village atmosphere. The streets were narrow and the brick sidewalks shaded by jacarandas and acacias. The architecture was predominantly Spanish, red tile and white stucco and brown adobe. New England colonial was also permitted, but modern was not and "high rise" was an epithet. However, the multi-storied monsters of glass and stainless steel, hotels and apartments, were beginning to change the skyline north of the river; the first shopping center had opened there last year. Everyone admitted that charm must give way to progress —it was as inevitable as the smog which crept closer from Los Angeles day by day—but Orchestra Beach continued to fight a stubborn delaying action.

The *Dispatch* was located at 437 Presidio Street, near the center of the downtown area. The forward third of the Moorish style building, once a grocery store, had been remodeled into offices and newsroom where the paper was written. The remaining two-thirds was the plant in which it was published. Since tidiness and journalism are mutually exclusive, both were cluttered, mainly with machinery that ranged from typewriters and duplicators to linotypes and the bulky rotary press. The *Dispatch* staff consisted of a managing editor, a secretary, an advertising salesman and two printers, all full-time employees, plus nearly as many part-time employees: a pair of housewives with journalistic ambitions who handled society and features, a photographer who operated his own studio, and a student from the university who moonlighted as circulation manager. Paul could, and sometimes did, fill in for any of them, including the printers. But his main function was executive since, as in any business, it was harder to find someone capable of making decisions than those capable of carrying them out.

Tom Easley was waiting to demand one the moment he entered the newsroom. "I was wondering how you want to handle the Victor Vandamm story." Easley had spent over thirty of his fifty years in the newspaper business (he called it "game" and loved it as such). Though nominally the managing editor, he wrote ninety per cent of the copy, rewrote most of the other ten per cent, and would have been a valuable addition to any metropolitan city room. Paul counted himself fortunate that a heart condition had made Easley seek the slower pace of Orchestra Beach.

"What Victor Vandamm story, Tom? Is there one?"

"Haven't you heard? He hanged himself last night in his apartment."

"Vandamm committed suicide? I can't believe it. Why?"

"God only knows—because Vandamm didn't leave a note. I agree it doesn't add up, not on the surface, anyway. I'd love to dig into it, but in view of the fact that Vandamm was a friend of yours and a wheel at Keller Corp besides—"

"I hardly knew the guy, actually. We played tennis a couple of times at the club, that's all. Sibby knew him a little better than I, through IBS, but I don't think Vandamm had any real friends. No reason to soft-pedal the story on our account—or Hank's, for that matter." Paul hesitated. "By the same token, there's no reason to hit it too hard, either, considering it's the Fiesta edition."

"Sure," Easley said ruefully. "Mustn't give the foreigners the wrong impression of our little paradise. Okay, we'll play it as straight news. Two inches on page twelve."

Paul patted his shoulder. "The cardinal rule of small circulation journalism, Tom. Boost, don't knock. Maybe that means compromising sometimes. On the other hand, maybe some oddball's suicide isn't worth more than two inches, anyway."

Wynne Rossi stuck her blonde head out of the next office. "Phone for you, Paul. Line one."

His caller was Hal Blum, who handled advertising for Hudson's, Orchestra Beach's oldest department store and the *Dispatch*'s largest account. Blum was upset. "I know you're a busy boy these days, Paul, but you promised me the corrected page proofs by Monday at the latest and here it is Tuesday and—"

"You mean you don't have them? I gave them to Wynne yesterday morning with orders to get them to you immediately."

"She must have sent 'em by way of Timbuktu. They ain't here yet."

"I'll check it out and get back to you." He hung up and yelled for his secretary. "Wynne, what happened to the Hudson page proofs? Hal Blum claims they were never delivered."

"But that's imposs—" Her blue eyes widened and she put a hand to her mouth. "Oh, my gosh! I'll bet they're still sitting on my desk."

"What! Wynne, how could you pull a stupid trick like that?"

She flushed. "I'm sorry, Paul. I guess I had other things on my mind."

"That's great," he said sarcastically. Wynne Rossi had

lived in Orchestra Beach slightly less than a year and had been his secretary nearly as long. He had hired her with reservations—young women generally got married or pregnant or both just about the time you had them properly trained. Wynne showed no intention of doing either. She kept the books, handled the billing, supervised the classified section and answered the telephone. Paul had come to depend on her as his Girl Friday. Thus, her dereliction angered him more than it would have in another of whom he expected less. "It's a shame if business is interfering with your private life. Next time tell me—"

To his consternation, she burst into tears. She tried to speak between sobs; the only word he could make out was "unforgivable."

He moved awkwardly to comfort her, disconcerted as most men are by women's tears. "Aw, come on," he soothed. "It's not that bad. Anybody can make a mistake. Sorry if I yelled at you."

"I don't blame you. I deserve it." She drew a deep shaky breath. "Paul, I think I should quit."

"Over a little thing like this? Look, Wynne, I know I've been pretty much of an ogre lately, what with the Fiesta and all—"

"You're not an ogre! You're a perfectly wonderful boss, the best I've ever had. It's just that, well, there are personal reasons."

This could be interpreted as a request not to pry, but Paul sensed it was a cry for help instead. He took her firmly by the elbow. "Anybody who runs out on me has got to have a better excuse than that. I'll listen to yours over a drink."

She objected, not too convincingly, so he steered her out of the office, pausing to instruct Easily to dispatch the tardy page proofs posthaste, and across the street to The Stage Stop.

Wynne guessed that she wanted "just coffee," but he ordered screwdrivers instead. While waiting for them to be delivered, Paul studied her unhappy face. It was a pretty face normally, oddly girlish for a woman of twenty-six and a divorcée besides, but the soft blue eyes and gentle mouth accurately reflected her vulnerable nature. Wynne was one whom life's blows bruise rather than toughen, while bravely pretending otherwise. Sibby suspected that she had a crush on her boss and joked about being jealous of her. Paul took neither possibility seriously.

"Now let's hear it," he suggested. "But no more tears, please. They'll only dilute your drink, and it's weak enough already."

He got a tremulous smile and, after some hesitation, the story. The true source of Wynne's distress was her ex-husband, although not precisely yet her ex, since the final decree was still pending. The picture she painted of Fred Rossi was that of an amoral ne'er-do-well, charming but shallow. The marriage had been empty, or worse, yet Rossi had fought the divorce and had vowed to punish her for obtaining it. "He never really loved me, but he enjoyed owning me, like a dog he could beat." It was apparently more than a figure of speech; Wynne was plainly terrified of him. Without a family to protect her, she had fled her home in Northern California to escape his persecution. Now a friend with whom she continued to correspond had warned her that Rossi might have learned of her hiding place.

"I haven't been able to sleep since I got the letter," she concluded. "If Fred knows where I am, he'll follow me sure and—"

"Calm down," Paul advised, since she appeared on the verge of more tears. "Suppose he does show up. What can he do? You don't belong to him any more."

"You don't know him like I do. He'll find some way to

make trouble. That's why I think I'd better move on." She stared miserably at her cocktail. "I don't want to go. I hope you know that, Paul. I've been very happy here with the *Dispatch*—and everything."

"Then don't go. I'd hate to lose you." Her suddenly hopeful glance made him wonder if Sibby's suspicions weren't correct, after all, so he elaborated, "Good secretaries don't grow in trees. Even more importantly, you can't keep running forever. There comes a time when you have to make a stand—and Orchestra Beach is a good place to make it."

Wynne was silent for a while. Finally, she murmured, "All right, Paul. If you want me to stay, I will."

He decided he'd better choose his words carefully. "The decision's up to you. I'm just giving you a little brotherly advice. Stop letting Fred spook you. Find yourself an eligible young bachelor—the town is full of them—marry him and bury the past. Do that, and you'll be surprised how good life can be."

The hint was not lost on her; she summoned a faint smile. "Thanks—brother. But you can't imagine what it's like to wake up every morning wondering if today is the day that the past catches up with you. How can you possibly be happy with a sword hanging over your head all the time?"

"I've got one suggestion. Don't look up."

Sibby came by at five to pick him up for the abalone hunt. "Want to take the van, too?" she asked. "Or shall we go in one car?"

"Might as well ride together," Paul decided. The Towers, like most Southern California families, found two automobiles a necessity. The yellow Toyota was the family car, which meant that Sibby operated it most of the time.

The blue Econoline van legally belonged to the *Dispatch* and carried its name in gleaming gold letters on all four sides. However, Paul utilized it for his private transportation when the vehicle was not needed by the circulation department or for other business uses.

"The Beach & Tennis Club, Jeeves, and make it snappy. I got a heavy date with an aqualung." He eyed her pullover sweater and slacks questioningly. "No bathing suit? Or are you changing there?"

"I'm not going in. My period started this afternoon, darn it. But I can still handle the boat for you. You don't mind, do you, darling?"

"That your period started or that you're not going in? The answer is yes to both. I wish I'd known earlier. We could have called this evening off. Now I went and promised George I'd bring him some abalone and he's counting on it. You should have phoned me."

"I did phone you," Sibby replied with a touch of asperity. "First, you were at your Fiesta meeting. After that, I'm told, you were out guzzling cocktails with your secretary. So don't blame me. I tried."

"Let's not be catty, dear. I guzzled only in the line of duty. Wynne came a bit unglued this afternoon. She's having some personal problems and the poor kid needed a shoulder to cry on."

"How convenient that yours was available." She gave him a sidelong glance. "I don't know what Wynne's so-called personal problems amount to and I don't want to. But don't let yourself get involved in them, Paul. If it's problems you want, I can give you plenty."

"My involvement, such as it is, was purely selfish. Wynne was making noises like she might quit, and I don't want to have to break in a new secretary."

"Okay then, you're forgiven." But that reminded Sibby

of something else and she asked, "Did you hear about Victor Vandamm?"

"Yeah. Too bad."

"Personally, I never cared much for the man, what little I saw of him, but you can't help but feel sorry for anyone who's driven to a thing like that. Hank thought he had such a brilliant mind."

"Statistics prove that very few morons commit suicide."

"You don't suppose this will throw a monkey wrench into Hank's new project, do you? Vandamm was in charge of it, you know." Neither she nor Paul was certain what the project amounted to, other than it involved some kind of military hardware. Contract negotiations had kept Hank Keller commuting to and from Washington nearly every week for the past six months. "How terrible for Hank if something went wrong now! Marilyn tells me that this new whatever-it-is will either make or break Keller Corp."

"Marilyn dramatizes—or haven't you ever noticed?"

"Yes, I suppose she does. But I happen to know that Hank went pretty deeply in hock to get this thing off the ground. Marilyn was against it, but you know my brother, a born optimist and stubborn as a mule, besides." Sibby chuckled wryly. "Lucky he's such a genius, because he's sure a lousy businessman. I remember when we were kids, he was always conning me out of my allowance because he'd squandered his sending away for some scientific marvel that usually didn't work, anyway. Were you ever like that, Paul?"

"I never had a sister, much less an allowance. And in Prichard, Nebraska, we considered the dial telephone the last word in scientific marvels."

"I'd like to see Prichard," Sibby mused. "When are you going to take me there, Paul?"

"Our very next vacation. You'll love it. During the day we can count out-of-state licenses on Main Street and at night we can watch the soda jerk draw cherry Cokes at Will's Drugstore. Two dashes of syrup, one dash of flavor. In the meantime, we'll just have to suffer along in dull old Orchestra Beach."

"You have no intention of ever taking me to Prichard—or anywhere else," Sibby declared. "Because you are a smug, self-satisfied stick-in-the-mud."

"You know what?" Paul said. "I do believe you're right."

Their destination, the Beach & Tennis Club, was located on the estuary south of town. The clubhouse was a large white Victorian castle with long verandas, gabled roof and haphazard turrets. The ornate formal dining room and the golf course which trailed up the hillside were open to the public; the tennis courts and heated pool were not. The Beach & Tennis Club was less the hub of Orchestra Beach social life than in the past. Newer residents considered it an anachronism, and to some extent they were right since it harked back to an era when wealth and gentility were usually synonymous. Yet the club continued to be prized, perhaps for this very reason, although the membership these days was drawn largely from the middle class rather than the rich. They grumbled about the monthly dues (which were actually quite reasonable, considering) but paid them. Paul was not the only one who wrote them off as a business expense, in his case legitimately, since he sold nearly as much advertising across a tennis net or over a drink in the lounge as at the office.

Nearly three hours of daylight remained. The Pacific was an undulating sapphire carpet, speckled with diamonds of reflected sunshine, and the salt breeze was warm.

On the horizon, the fog—which had continued to linger unseasonably past its usual June departure—boded ill for later, but at this moment the beauty of the scene could scarcely have been improved on. "Gosh, we're lucky people!" Sibby murmured. "I'll get Dirty Gertie warmed up while you're changing."

Paul entered the boathouse, identical in architecture to the main building but a fraction of its size. Jerry, who ran it, was listening to the Dodger game on the radio. He was a club institution, a wiry man of fifty, tanned the color of English oak, who doubled as swimming coach and tennis instructor.

Paul's scuba gear was already lying on the counter. "Sibby phoned you were coming," Jerry explained. "What's it going to be today—abalone?"

Paul nodded. "How's the water, Jerr?"

"Seventy degrees. Slight chop. Should be ideal."

In the locker room Paul put on trunks, since the water temperature made a wet suit unnecessary, and buckled the weighted belt around his waist. He examined the pressure gauge to make sure his tanks had been serviced following his last dive; they had. He slung the harness over his shoulder, collected the balance of his equipment—swim fins, face mask and the tire iron with which to pry the tenacious abalone from the rocks—and went to rejoin Sibby.

The club's marina was crowded, with nearly every berth taken. Many of the boats were ocean-going craft, twenty-four-footers and above with inboard engines, outfitted like small homes and nearly as expensive. Their fourteen-foot outboard could have served some of the larger vessels as a lifeboat. Sibby had the engine idling smoothly. She was a good sailor, having spent her entire life adjacent to the water. It was she who had introduced her husband to the pleasures that could be experienced on its surface and beneath it.

"Darn it," she said, regarding him enviously. "I'd love to be going in with you. Why do I have to be a woman, anyway?"

"I wouldn't have it any other way. Cast off, Commodore."

They left the marina and headed down the estuary toward the open sea, keeping to the lee of the point which acted as a natural barrier against the swells rolling in across the Pacific. "About there," Paul said, pointing to a spot fifty yards offshore. "If memory serves."

Sibby silenced the engine, dropped anchor and assisted him in donning the scuba gear. "Be careful," she cautioned. "Since I'm not along to hold your hand."

"Yes, Mother. You stand by to haul up the bucket. I'll give two tugs on the line when it's full."

He slid over the side and ducked his head beneath the surface to check the breathing apparatus. Satisfied, he let the bucket fill with water; then, giving Sibby a salute with the tire iron, followed as it sank toward the bottom. As always, at that first moment of total immersion, he experienced exhilaration. The fins propelled him effortlessly into a silent kingdom where gravity was dethroned and infinite power was his.

The bucket came to rest on the bottom amid a jumble of rocks that resembled the ruins of an ancient fortress. The crumbled ramparts were festooned with plants among whose lacy tendrils darted small fish, vivid bits of color in the clear water. They scurried away from this larger fish which cruised above them, trailing bubbles as no fish should.

Paul watched them for a moment, wishing he could reassure them that they were not his prey, then began to search for the abalone which was. He was annoyed to see his face plate cloud up. What the hell was wrong with the . . . Suddenly he realized that it was his vision, not the

33

glass, that was at fault. The light was failing—had the fog moved in more quickly than they anticipated, covering the sun? He began to feel strangely lightheaded and vaguely disoriented. Need more air, he thought, fumbling with the valve. And found himself unable to turn it; his fingers were like sausages, flabby and without strength. At the same instant, his lungs commenced to burn although the air flowed as freely into the mouthpiece as before. Panic swept through him. My God, he was drowning! Fish no longer but a terrified trespasser in a hostile world, he shed harness, tanks and belt—the tire iron had fallen from his hands already, when he wasn't sure—and clawed frantically toward the surface.

Or was it toward the surface? He could no longer tell. He knew only that his consciousness was fading and that his life would follow. Something brushed across his face. Though he was unable to bring it into focus, he realized that it must be the line secured to the bucket. And, much more importantly, to Sibby's wrist.

Frenzied hands were tugging at his armpits and a terrified voice was calling his name. But all that really mattered was the air—the sweet, marvelous life-giving air—that filled his aching lungs. The darkness retreated. He made out Sibby's face close to his. She had plunged into the sea, fully clothed, to rescue him.

He tried to tell her that he was all right but she ordered him not to speak and helped him drag himself into the boat. She followed and they sat there, staring dumbly at each other and panting with exhaustion and relief.

At last she whispered, "Paul—what on earth happened?"

"Don't know. I started to feel funny, then things got fuzzy and I must have passed out."

"I felt you tug on the line and I started to haul in. Next thing I knew I could see you coming up. You looked so limp and—and—" She began to cry. "Oh, God, darling— I thought you were dead!"

He was too drained to do more than pat her knee weakly. "Not quite. But if you hadn't been here . . . Can't figure what went wrong, though. I was getting air but I still couldn't seem to breathe."

"It's my fault," Sibby said in bitter self-condemnation. "All my life it's been dinned into me: Never, never, never dive alone. And I sat right here and let you. I even encouraged you to go! Oh, Paul, if anything had happened to you!"

His strength was returning rapidly; he was able to kiss her and even to attempt a pallid joke. "Thought you could get out of going swimming, huh?"

Sibby shivered. She was wetter than he, since skin dried faster than fabric. "I've got to get you back. No, you rest —I'll handle the boat."

Nor would she permit him to leave the dock, once they reached it, ordering him to wait while she fetched Jerry to help. Paul allowed her to have her way. It was good to sit quietly and absorb the wonder of being live. Death was the ultimate certainty, of course, but only on a dim and distant "someday." He could not quite comprehend that this placid sunny afternoon had come close to being his "someday."

Sibby returned on the run, bringing with her not only Jerry but another man in white tennis shorts who carried a leather valise. She introduced him breathlessly as "Doctor Stevenson, who just happened to be here."

"I'm just a little winded," Paul protested. "I don't need a doctor."

"Your wife thinks you may have suffered a heart attack," Stevenson explained, a possibility which Paul hadn't even considered. "It won't hurt to check." He proceeded with a swift and practiced examination. "No cardiac history, you say? Well, your pulse is a bit rapid, which is only natural. But it's strong and regular and your lungs seem clear also. I can't find anything to worry about. I would recommend an EKG, though, just as a routine precaution. How old are you—about thirty? Might as well face the fact that you're not the man you were ten years ago. None of us are." He brushed away their expressions of gratitude and strode back toward the tennis courts.

Her fears assuaged, Sibby regarded Jerry grimly. "Then it was the equipment. What have you been doing with Paul's tanks, anyway?"

"What I always do. Fill and check them."

"Well, you must have forgotten—or something."

"Now wait a minute," Jerry replied indignantly. "I know you're upset and I don't blame you, but if you think that I—"

Paul quelled the argument. "Nobody's blaming you, Jerry. I checked the pressure and flow myself and the tanks were full, all right. But I'm pretty sure that whatever it was that I was getting wasn't air. Could somebody have tapped the $CO_2$ by mistake?"

"Hell, no. I filled them myself—" Jerry hesitated. "No, I take that back. I usually fill the members' tanks personally except I got so busy this week that I gave the job to the klutz I had working for me. But I remember sitting him down right beside the compressed air cylinder. I don't see how he could have goofed it. We keep the $CO_2$ on the other side of the boathouse."

"I'd like a word with Mr. Klutz," Sibby said between her teeth.

"He quit yesterday." Jerry shrugged. "I'm having a hell

of a time keeping help. These surf bums drift in, looking for a soft touch, then move on when they find out I expect them to work. This Johnson character was the third one in the past month."

Jerry had no idea where Johnson had gone—or where he had come from, for that matter—and although Sibby vowed to have him arrested, Paul told her to forget it. "We couldn't prove anything without the tanks. They're at the bottom of the estuary and they'll be empty by now, anyway. Might as well chalk it up to experience."

"Somebody ought to be made to pay for it," Sibby grumbled. However, she could not decide who or how, and Jerry mollified her somewhat by volunteering to retrieve the abandoned scuba gear. Yet as they walked back to their car, she said thoughtfully, "Maybe we should take this as a warning and give up diving. You know what the doctor said. You're not as young as you used to be."

"A penetrating remark, if ever I heard one. Let's not hit the panic button, honey. If I'd had an accident in the car, would you suggest I give up driving?"

"All I'm saying is you don't have to go looking for trouble."

"One thing I've noticed about trouble. You get it whether you look for it or not. But stop worrying. I'm awfully good at ducking."

Wife-like, Sibby made him swear that he would have the EKG "the first thing in the morning," but, husband-like, he reneged. By morning the near tragedy had receded, losing much of its terror. Paul felt fine and Sibby, suffering from menstrual cramps and a splitting headache, accepted his excuse that he was much too rushed to visit a doctor today. It was more than an alibi. The Fiesta, which had seemed so far in the future all these past months, was now almost upon him, bringing with it the plethora of last-minute details which could no longer be postponed. When George phoned to inquire about the abalone, Paul wasn't even able to spare the time to explain fully why he had failed to make good on his promise. "Give the girl chili and beans," he suggested. "I know you're a whiz with those."

"Big thrill," George said, disgruntled. "Didn't I mention that she happens to be Mexican?"

Paul had his own problems to worry about. The special Fiesta edition of the *Dispatch* ran to double the normal number of pages, sixteen instead of eight. The advertising had not increased in the same proportion, which meant that more copy was required. Tom Easley, although a facile reporter, could not be expected to produce it all. Paul spent the day writing stories and heads, correcting galley proofs and preparing page dummies, with frequent interruptions to answer requests from the other news media— radio and television and the metropolitan newspapers—for information on the Fiesta. He was glad to see quitting time arrive.

When he went out to the van, he found Wynne sitting in her Volkswagen, its starter grinding away impotently. "I don't know what's wrong," she said. "It was fine this morning."

"Probably flooded," Paul decided after checking to make sure there was fuel in the tank. However, he couldn't coax ignition from the engine either, although the electrical system seemed to be working, nor did tinkering with the carburetor help. "Guess you need a mechanic," he finally admitted. "Where do you usually take it?"

"That garage over on Mission that specializes in foreign cars. Except that it's nearly six and they close at five-thirty."

Why did automobiles invariably break down after business hours? "Okay, hop in the van and I'll drive you home. You can have them pick it up in the morning."

Wynne hated to impose but not enough to refuse his offer. Besides, she wanted to talk. "Thanks again for straightening me out yesterday," she told him as they drove. "I don't know what I'd have done without you."

"All I did was listen."

"You did more than that—much more. You cared. You're a nice man, Paul. There's only one thing wrong with you."

"Bad breath?"

"You should be twins. Either that or . . ." She bit her lip and didn't finish the sentence.

Paul guessed that "single" was the word she had left unspoken. It seemed to him also that Wynne was sitting a trifle closer to him than necessary. Feeling himself on dangerous ground, he invoked his wife's name for protection. "Sibby wouldn't agree with you. She thinks that one of me is plenty."

Wynne lived north of the shopping center amid the apartment complexes that had sprung up within the past three years. Hers was one of the less pretentious structures, middle-income housing lacking the patio or pool that many boasted, and designed to appeal to young couples without children or older couples whose children had grown. Its principal attraction, aside from the modest rent, was expressed in the name: Seaview. "Nice place," Paul commented, although he considered it rather ordinary.

So did Wynne. "It's a place. We do have our own parking, at least. Some of the other apartments—"

"Parking!" he said suddenly, and swore. "I knew I'd forgotten something. Osborn asked me to call Sergeant Lupo today to check on off-street parking for the Fiesta. It completely slipped my mind until this minute. Is there a phone booth around here—a gas station, maybe?"

"Why not use mine? I'd like you to see the apartment, anyway." She noticed his hesitation and her mouth quirked. "Of course, if you feel you shouldn't . . ."

He decided that refusing would give the situation more importance than it warranted. Wynne directed him to her numbered stall at the foot of the stairs. "The manager screams bloody murder if we take somebody else's space." The parking lot was on the street side, as was the open staircase that led to the balconies on which the apartments opened. This arrangement permitted the windows to be located on the west elevation, affording the advertised view of the Pacific.

Her apartment was on the third floor. Paul accompanied her up the two flights with a vague uneasiness. There was nothing wrong with using his secretary's telephone. Sibby would certainly understand (she would, wouldn't she?) but, all the same, he hoped that nobody he knew would see him. He found himself talking in a louder than normal voice to demonstrate that there was nothing illicit about his visit.

Yet he could not restrain a furtive backward glance before following Wynne through the doorway. For that reason he was unaware that the room was already occupied until he heard her shriek. Turning his head quickly in alarm, he saw an indistinct figure rushing toward him. "You son of a bitch!" a male voice yelled. At virtually the same instant a fist struck him squarely on the mouth.

Paul lurched back, more bewildered than hurt. He put up his hands instinctively to ward off a second blow. There was none; Wynne forced herself between the two men. "Fred!" she cried. "Stop it! Leave him alone, do you hear me?"

"Like hell," the man growled, attempting to thrust her aside. "I'll teach the bastard to screw around with my wife."

"Get out of the way, Wynne," Paul ordered. Outrage replaced confusion; he tasted blood and didn't intend to bleed alone. "I'm ready for him now."

Wynne, shaking her head frantically, refused to move. After a moment Paul realized that the man she called Fred—and who could only be Fred Rossi, her divorced husband—didn't really want her to. Sneak attacks were apparently more to his liking. With surprise no longer on his side, he was content to rely on bluster. He continued to glare at Paul while he allowed Wynne to push him away. "Okay, okay. I'll take it easy on the boy friend." He turned and swaggered across the living room to the small bar.

Now it was Paul whom Wynne held back, her palms against his chest. "Please, Paul," she begged. "For my sake. Please don't make things worse than they already are."

"He's a lover, not a fighter," Rossi sneered, filling a tumbler with Scotch. However, he continued to hold the bottle in case Paul attempted to prove him wrong. "You're lucky I didn't shoot you, crumb. I got every right to. There's such a thing as the unwritten law, you know."

Paul felt reasonably confident that he could whip the other man. He was Rossi's equal in both height and weight and obviously his superior in courage, since Rossi had felt it necessary to arm himself with the bottle. Yet he recognized that continuing the scuffle would cause more trouble than it cured. Prudence overcame anger. "All right," he told Wynne. "We'll let it go for now."

Feeling himself out of danger, Rossi uttered a derisive laugh. "Any time, crumb." The boast was patently hollow, as was the man who uttered it. Paul, who had learned to judge character quickly, sized him up as a con artist with more gall than guts. Women, his natural prey, might consider Rossi handsome—his dark curly hair, long sideburns and mustache bore a superficial resemblance to Paul himself, in fact—but the sly eyes and vain mouth would cause men to dismiss him as a weakling, although a vicious one.

Wynne faced her former husband wrathfully. "What are you doing here? And how did you get in? That door was locked."

Rossi chose to answer the least important question. "I looked for the key under the mat where you always keep it. I know you pretty damn well, sweetheart. By the way, aren't you going to introduce me to lover boy?"

"Mr. Towers is my boss. I'm his secretary and that's all I am."

"Sure you are. You know what they say about a secretary—she's not a fixture at the office until she's been screwed on the desk. Though I guess this is a nicer arrangement." He surveyed the apartment with exaggerated approval. "Pretty sweet little love nest you've got here."

"It isn't a love nest! Mr. Towers just stopped by to use the phone."

"Right! A five-buck phone call—or do the rates go down after six p.m.?"

Wynne flushed. "Get out of here! We're not married any longer. I don't have to take your insults. Get out or I'll call the police."

"Maybe that's not such a bad idea." The threat didn't faze him; he had doubtless heard it before, both from Wynne and other women. "We can have a long chat with the fuzz, the three of us. I got nothing to hide. How does that grab you, Mr. Towers?"

It didn't grab Paul in the slightest, but he knew he would be unwise to admit it. "I'll be glad to talk to the police. I don't have anything to hide, either."

Rossi's bluff worked on Wynne, however. Her resolution wavered, then collapsed. "Oh, what's the use?" she muttered. "He'd just lie the way he always does, turn black into white. Paul, you'd better leave. This is my mess, not yours. There's no reason you should get mixed up in it."

Paul could hardly agree more. Yet pride—and the fact that he felt sorry for Wynne—prevented his leaping at the suggestion. "I'll stick around if you want me to."

"No, I can handle things." She urged him toward the door. "I'm sorry, Paul. I wouldn't have had this happen for the world."

"Hey, crumb!" Rossi called after him. "Stay away from my wife if you know what's good for you, kapeesh?"

On the balcony Paul paused to straighten his tie, put askew in the brief struggle. "Jesus!" he murmured. "How did I get into that, anyway?" As on the previous afternoon, he had done nothing to invite trouble, yet trouble had found him. Nor had his claim of being a good ducker proved entirely accurate. The inside of his mouth was bleeding from Rossi's punch. Using his handkerchief to wipe the blood from his lips, he hurried down the stairs to the van and headed home. He drove carefully, as befitting a man who fears he may be accident-prone.

"Stop your blubbering," Fred Rossi said contemptuously. "I didn't slap you that hard. It was just a love pat, baby."

Wynne continued to cower on the sofa where he had flung her. "Why won't you leave me alone?" she whimpered. "What did I ever do to you?"

"You ran away," he explained in the patient tone one might employ to chide a naughty child. "You know how much you mean to me and still you ran away."

"You don't love me! You never did!"

"Sounds like you've become quite an expert on love. Towers must be a good teacher." He shook his head with mock sorrow. "You've been a wicked little girl, Wynne. Lucky for you that I'm the forgiving type."

"There's nothing between Mr. Towers and me—"

"I thought you called him Paul."

"All right—between Paul and me. He's just the man I work for."

"For or under? Don't try to con me, Wynne. I saw how you looked at him with those baby-blue eyes. You're hung on him." He watched her expression. "You figure you're rid of dear old Fred and here's a good-looking bird with plenty of scratch—so why not?"

"It's not like that at all. I'll admit I like Paul because he's fine and generous and good—and, yes, if he wasn't married—"

"What's married got to do with it? I haven't met a husband yet who won't go for a little extracurricular nooky if he thinks he can get away with it." He raised a placating hand. "I know, I know. It's all been strictly platonic with you and him."

"It has! I swear to you, Fred."

"And I believe you, baby. I wonder if Mrs. Towers would, though."

Wynne sat up quickly. "Are you hinting that you might tell her?"

"How could I—when there's nothing to tell? I don't believe in breaking up a happy home, anyhow. Live and let live, that's me." He paused. "Of course, what with the

44

high cost of living these days . . . well, a man has got to look out for himself."

"You try to blackmail Paul," Wynne said furiously, "and I'll—I'll kill you! I mean it, Fred."

"Did I say anything about blackmail? You've sure got a low opinion of me, Wynne. Guess I'm going to have to show you that I'm really a very lovable guy." He held out his arms, fingers beckoning. "Come here."

She cringed away. "What do you want?"

"If you've been as faithful to me as you make out, you must be pretty pent-up by now. I know I am. It's been— let's see—damn near a year, hasn't it?"

Her voice was hoarse with fright and loathing. "If you dare touch me, I'll scream!"

"No, you won't," he replied in a tone of quiet menace, moving closer. "You're going to be as sweet as pie to me, sweetie pie. Because if you aren't, I might feel compelled to do something that you and Mr. Towers wouldn't like, not one little bit." He pulled her up to face him. "You can fight some if you want," he told her. "I like it better that way."

On the way home, Paul tried to decide how he would tell Sibby. As an amusing anecdote? ("A funny thing happened to me today on the way to . . .") Except that it hadn't been amusing, nor would Sibby consider it so. As casual dinner-table conversation? ("Oh, by the way, I got into a little fight this evening and . . .") That didn't sound too promising either. No matter how he phrased the story, it had the ring of a confession. Damn it, he was innocent of any wrongdoing! The trick was to make Sibby believe it.

The Towers lived on the hillside east of town, not amid

the expensive homes that commanded the heights but on the lower-priced slopes below. Theirs was a tract home, one among a group with basically the same floor plan but made distinct from its neighbors by different exterior elevations. The architecture was Southern California ranch modern, so-called for its split shake roof and rough board-and-batten walls with an occasional touch of used brick. It had the advantage of being situated on a cul-de-sac between two small canyons, setting it and the four other dwellings which shared Cabrillo Court apart from the rest of the subdivision. Paul and Sibby considered themselves fortunate to live there, although Sibby spoke of wanting a larger place "eventually." In the meantime, Paul had built a patio and a laundry room and had plans for converting the third bedroom into a den. Or nursery, if Sibby had her way.

Paul rarely turned into the cul-de-sac without experiencing a feeling of well-being, the knight returning from the wars. This evening he approached his castle with a certain apprehension. The fair damsel within had a temper and he was far from convinced that she would view his saga tolerantly. "Might as well tell her right away and get it over with," he muttered. "She'll understand."

His reception was not encouraging. "Where in the world have you been?" Sibby cried. "Do you know what time it is?"

The question was rhetorical but he answered it, anyway. "It's only six forty-five."

"You're usually home hours ago," she said with wifely exaggeration. "And to be late tonight of all nights—"

"Why of all nights?"

"Because we're invited to Hank and Marilyn's for dinner and we're supposed to be there at seven and you're not even dressed."

Paul realized tardily that she was wearing a party gown of filmy dacron rather than her usual stay-at-home smock. "I'm sorry," he apologized stiffly, feeling that her annoyance was unmerited (and hadn't this turned out to be a lousy day, though!). "How was I to know?"

"Well, I expected you home at the regular time. When you didn't arrive and didn't arrive, I finally phoned your office and Tom told me that you'd gone off with Wynne again."

"Her car broke down and I gave her a ride home." He hesitated, wondering if he should elaborate.

"That woman certianly has more than her share of trouble," Sibby snapped. "What would she ever do if you weren't around to bail her out, I wonder? I don't know about you, but I'm getting a wee bit tired of it, Paul."

He decided that now was not the propitious moment. "I'll try to see that it doesn't happen again." He gave her a peck on the cheek. "Uh—how you feeling, hon?"

"Better than I did earlier. I still have this rotten headache, though."

"Then why are we going out? I'm pretty bushed myself. Call Hank and Marilyn and ask for a rain check."

"It's important that we go," Sibby said, rather oddly. "You'll find out why later." She pushed him toward the bedroom. "Hurry and get changed. You don't have to shower, do you? I'll phone Marilyn and tell her we'll be a little late."

"Okay," he grumbled. "If we must, we must. But I hope that Hank doesn't lap up all the booze before we get there. The day I've had, I sure could use a drink."

The Keller estate (no one in the family ever called it by such a pretentious name; it was merely "our place") occupied a promontory with the best view in Orchestra

Beach; some said on the entire coast. When the atmospheric conditions were right, you could see all the way from La Jolla on the south to Point Fermin on the north and the offshore islands—Catalina and San Clemente—appeared near enough to touch. Sibby's grandfather had acquired the property in the early days, had built the house which stood there and planted the pine trees that shaded it. Hank and Marilyn admitted that the rambling old mansion, remodeled and expanded over the years, was impractical to maintain. However, the three-acre yard was ideal for children, of which they had five. The grounds were continually overrun by animals—ranging from dogs and cats to hawks and turtles—the driveway often blocked by one or more old jalopies in various stages of reconstruction, while the human traffic that flowed in and out would have kept an airport control tower busy. Sibby vowed that such a cluttered household would drive her wild and wondered how Marilyn stood it. But Marilyn thrived amid the confusion and her husband didn't even appear to be aware of it.

They entertained as casually as they lived. When Paul and Sibby arrived, Hank Keller was barbecuing steaks on the spacious bricked patio. Marilyn lay in the hammock, strumming on the guitar that was her latest enthusiasm. Paul and Sibby were overdressed in comparison to their hosts. Hank wore shorts and sneakers without socks, while Marilyn was garbed in denim jeans and a man-tailored shirt; her feet were bare. She gave them a smile and a "Hi, you-all" but did not stop her playing. That was Marilyn; she scorned formality as she scorned make-up. She was handsome without it—a big graceful woman, placid in disposition and boundless in energy.

She was, everyone agreed, the perfect wife for Hank who needed (and freely admitted it) a woman who could keep his life on an even keel. Hank was as different from his sister as two persons can possibly be, sloppy where she was fastidious, easy-going where she was intense. There was not even a familial resemblance between the hulking man and the petite woman. Despite this, a strong attachment bound them closer together than most brothers and sisters. Even more surprising—since they too were opposites and there was no kinship of blood—a similar bond existed between the brothers-in-law.

Hank waved away their apologies. "When were you ever on time, Sis? I spent half my young life fuming outside the bathroom door."

"I'm the culprit this evening," Paul said. "I was late getting home from the office."

"Fix yourself a drink. You've got some catching up to do. Hey, good people, shake hands with Joe Chalk. Joe—Paul and Sibby."

Paul had not been aware of the other guest present. It was difficult to understand, since Chalk was too big a man to be easily overlooked. Perhaps it was his way of standing completely motionless, scarcely appearing to breathe, which made him blend into the background. Or perhaps it was his neutral coloring, muted browns and grays like a bird's protective plumage. Yet if Chalk were a bird, it was an eagle or a falcon; his face was gaunt and predatory and his hazel eyes lacked warmth. The fingers that closed on Paul's were like talons.

"Glad to meet you." His voice matched the rest of him, low-keyed and harsh. "Hank's been telling me all about you."

"That's too bad," Paul replied, smiling. "I'll try to change your opinion."

The humor did not register with Chalk. "He thinks very highly of you." He regarded Paul as if seeking to learn why, then turned to Sibby with a polite remark about the weather.

Paul poured cocktails, a small one for Sibby, a much larger one for himself. "Where are the kids?" he asked Marilyn.

"I fed them early and they took off in five different directions. They didn't say where and I didn't dare ask. Don't tell me you miss having them under your feet and in your hair."

"Well, Sibby led me to believe that this is some sort of family celebration, so naturally I expected . . ."

"There are family celebrations—and there are family celebrations," Marilyn said enigmatically.

Before he could pursue the matter, Hank called "Come and get it!" and Paul was compelled to repress his curiosity. Nor did the conversation at the meal, eaten picnic-style at the redwood table, dwell on any but the most ordinary topics. He learned (from Hank, not the taciturn Chalk) that the Kellers' other guest had recently arrived from Washington, D.C., that he was staying at the Outrigger Motel, and that he neither contemplated remaining long nor departing soon. Paul concluded that he must have some connection with Keller Corp's new government contract.

"Say," he remarked to Hank during a lull in the conversation, "I was sorry to hear about Vandamm. I know it must have hit you pretty hard."

"I'll get over it," Hank said in a surprisingly indifferent voice, uncharacteristic of a man whose sympathies were easily stirred as a rule. "More steak, anyone? There's plenty left."

"Save room for dessert," Marilyn cautioned. "Cheesecake, Paul, your favorite."

So much for Victor Vandamm; the suicide of Hank

Keller's right-hand man was not touched upon again. Paul, who was quick to catch nuances, wondered if the presence of Joe Chalk had something to do with Hank's reluctance to discuss the tragedy. Well, it was none of his business, certainly.

After coffee, Marilyn asked Sibby if she would like to look at the new drapes and led her into the house, leaving the three men alone on the patio. There was a short silence, then Hank cleared his throat. "Guess we can get down to cases now," he said and glanced for confirmation at Chalk, who nodded. "Got a little matter I want to discuss with you, Paul."

His serious expression, combined with the hints the women had dropped earlier, confirmed Paul's hunch that this was not the spur-of-the-moment get-together he had first supposed. "Discuss ahead."

"How much do you know about the project Keller Corp's working on now?" Paul confessed his ignorance. "Then let me fill you in. See that down there?" Hank pointed at the shimmering blue waters of the Pacific. "That's a mighty important hunk of real estate. Some of the best military minds think that the oceans have more strategic value even than space. In case of an atomic war, God forbid, the sea may be the difference between victory or defeat—or life and death. That's why our government is pushing hard on underwater research. You remember that I was involved in the Sealab project. Well, Sealab didn't meet all its goals, but it did prove that man is able to create an artificial environment on the ocean bottom where he can live and work. Someday we may be able to build whole cities under the sea. We may have to if we keep mucking up the atmosphere. But that's only a long-range possibility. The here and now is strictly military. I'm giving away no secrets when I tell you that the Pentagon has blueprinted a number of ICBM and ABM installations along the continental shelf, Atlantic as well as Pacific. They can be made movable rather than stationary and they have a great advantage over our present fixed silo system because they'd be tough as hell for the enemy to knock out by a surprise attack. This country has followed a strategy of nuclear deterrent—keep the Reds from hitting us because they know we'll be able to hit back. Given Russia's present missile-orbiting capability—where they might be able to neutralize our ICBMs before we could activate—that strategy gets weaker by the hour. For that reason, the undersea platform is a must."

He paused to refill his coffee cup. Paul asked, "Are you telling me that Keller Corp is building these platforms?"

"Nope. I'd love to have the contract, but we're not big enough to handle it. Our part in the program is much, much smaller. Smaller—but vital. The platforms have one unfortunate weak spot."

"Submarine attack?"

"Right you are. We can hide our platforms beneath the waves, but the enemy can hide his subs there, too. Our detection system leaves a lot to be desired. It's nowhere near as advanced or reliable as our radar, for instance. One of the Navy's top priority items over the last five years has been to develop a more sophisticated sonar. Some pretty good men have tried and failed."

"But you've come up with it," Paul murmured. "Congratulations, Hank."

"We may have achieved a break-through," Hank agreed with typical scientific caution. "The tests have been encouraging, enough so that Washington has given us the green light to set up a pilot program. We call it SWORD—for Subsurface Warning, Observation, Ranging and Detection. I know, that's pretty cute, but it's better than 'the thing.' I won't confuse you with the technical aspects except to say that it's based on the pulsed-gas laser principle, with some important modifications. We believe that SWORD will operate effectively up to one hundred miles, which is over three times farther than anybody's best to date. With that sort of range, we could make the platforms pretty near impregnable. SWORD has other possibilities too, not all of them military. Locating schools of fish, charting currents, that sort of thing. You can see why I'm excited about it."

"I sure can. You may wind up as the family's first millionaire." Paul grinned. "Am I wrong in assuming that all this is not for publication?"

Chalk entered the conversation for the first time. "It wouldn't matter too much if you did print it. The Soviets already know as much as Hank has told you. Matter of fact, they know a damn sight more. They know that SWORD exists and what it can do. What they don't know —yet—is how it does it. They're busting their balls to get their hands on it."

"You mean they've tried to steal it? How?"

"Victor Vandamm," Chalk said, making the name sound like an obscenity.

Hank noted Paul's incredulous expression. "I know. Cloak-and-dagger shenanigans in Orchestra Beach are a bit much to swallow. But there isn't any doubt about it. Vandamm sold out."

"To whom—the Russians?"

"Have you ever heard of the KGB, Mr. Towers?"

"Isn't that a radio station down in San Diego?"

Hank smiled; Chalk did not. "The KGB is the Soviet equivalent of our FBI and CIA, only bigger. They run a worldwide operation. Mr. Hoover estimates that there may be as many as three thousand KGB agents in the United States. This area draws more than its share because you're topheavy with defense work."

"Vandamm wasn't actually a Red agent," Hank explained. "More their patsy. It appears there was a homosexual angle we weren't aware of—and they used that to force him to feed them information on SWORD. Luckily, Joe's people got wind of it before Vandamm could do much real damage."

"Joe's people," Paul repeated. "That would be the FBI, wouldn't it?"

"Why not the CIA?" Chalk parried.

"Well, I noticed that you put the FBI first. And you referred to the boss as 'Mr.' Hoover."

"Not bad," Chalk admitted. "Yes, it's FBI, Mr. Towers. We've been watching Vandamm for the past couple of months. We could have picked him up at any time, but we were hoping he'd lead us to his employers. Vandamm learned that we were zeroing in on him. The bastard hanged himself rather than face the music."

"Poor guy," Paul murmured. "Caught in the middle and no way out. He must have gone through hell."

"Save your sympathy for those who deserve it, not some gutless fairy. And you're wrong, he did have a way out. We could have struck some sort of bargain. Dead, he's a total loss."

"Then I gather you haven't had much luck uncovering the real agents, the people Vandamm was working for."

"No, damn it. We bugged his apartment and read his mail. Nothing. Vandamm didn't have any close friends, but we've checked out all his acquaintances, anyone he ever spoke to more than once, including the milkman." Chalk hesitated. "Even you, Mr. Towers. You played tennis with him a couple of times, I believe. We came up empty all around."

Paul whistled softly. "I'll be more careful about my choice of partners from now on."

"Me too," Hank said ruefully. "I thought I had a jewel in Victor. His track record back East was the greatest. Of course, he'd only been with Keller Corp since March, but I was completely sold on him. Makes you wonder if you can trust anybody. I've even been giving Marilyn the suspicious eye lately. By the way," he added, "I haven't breathed one word to her about this business. Don't you tell Sibby, either. No use worrying the girls—and the fewer people who know, the better."

"Sure. But since secrecy is the order of the day, why are you telling me?"

"The Vandamm mess has raised serious doubts back in Washington about Keller Corp. Whether we're able to handle a top-secret project such as SWORD. I can't say that I blame them. I've always run the business pretty much out of my hat. I'll be the first to admit that organization isn't my strong suit. Since Washington is convinced that the Soviets will make another attempt to get SWORD, they're demanding a complete overhaul of our systems and procedures before we go into production. What's needed is a topflight executive, a man who can take over the management end and tie the loose ends together. And, of course, a man who can be trusted absolutely. It's a hell of a big job. The man who can handle it should be able to write his own ticket. Salary, stock options, maybe even a partnership—you name it."

His meaning was obvious, but Paul asked the question anyway. "You're not offering me the job, are you?"

"You said I was going to be the family's first millionaire." Hank grinned. "How would you like to be the second?"

They drove home in a silence which Paul finally broke. "You mad at me, honey?"

"Why should I be?" Sibby replied stiffly. Which meant that she was, very. A moment later, she confirmed it. "It's simply that I can't understand why you didn't jump at Hank's proposition. I never was so shocked in my life—and particularly after I'd as much as promised Marilyn over the phone that you'd be thrilled to death."

"Maybe you should have discussed the matter with me first."

"Did you discuss your refusal with me first?" she retorted.

He couldn't rebut the feminine logic. "Well, that's neither here nor there. Anyway, I didn't refuse. I promised I'd think it over."

"That amounts to the same thing. I know you. Or at least I thought I did. Now I wonder. Any man who'd turn down the chance of a lifetime—"

"Did it ever occur to you that I'm happy right where I am, running the *Dispatch?* It's not exactly the worst job in the world, you know."

"Oh, please!" Sibby said wearily. "You're not going into the I'm-a-born-newspaperman-with-ink-in-my-veins-instead-of-blood speech, are you? You've told me dozens of times that it was just a business to you and that's all. Sure, you've done famously with the *Dispatch* and I'm not complaining—but we both know that it never will amount to much more than it does right now, a small paper in a small town. This new job, on the other hand—"

"I know, I know. There's millions in it!"

"I hope you don't believe that it's just the money I'm thinking of. I'm thinking of you, Paul. You work hard, harder than any man I know. Why shouldn't you put all that sweat to some real use—in a job that's worthy of your talents? Selling advertising . . . there must be thousands of men who can do that. But there aren't many men who could run Keller Corp. You could, it's right up your alley.

Anyway," she went on, "what's so wrong with money, for that matter? We'd be able to do some of the things we've dreamed about—including starting our family."

"Okay. I admit that everything you say is true."

"Then why on earth—"

"Maybe I've got a thing against the job itself. I couldn't tell Hank this without offending him, and he's too grand a guy for that, but you know how I feel about the armaments race, the insane way we're all escalating tensions until finally . . . Every new weapon—and you'll notice they're always labeled defensive—contributes to the madness. There's not much I can do to stop it. But I don't have to be part of it, either."

"I appreciate your principles, but—"

"As long as I don't put them into practice. Is that what you mean?"

"What I mean is, I think that you're being rather ridiculous applying them to this situation. Good Lord, you're not being asked to build a cobalt bomb or manufacture napalm! You admit you admire my brother. Do you think he'd be involved in anything immoral?"

"Morality is something that everyone has to decide for himself. Hank's doing what he believes right. All I ask is the freedom to do the same."

"Then you never had any intention of accepting his offer, did you?" His silence was her answer. "I thought so."

"I'm not sure I could handle the job, anyway," Paul added as he turned the car into their driveway. "All of you claim I could do it with one hand tied behind my back—but suppose you're wrong? I've never run anything the size of Keller Corp. Better to be a big frog in a small puddle, et cetera."

"I didn't know I was marrying a frog," Sibby snapped. "I supposed I was marrying a handsome prince."

She went into the house and directly to their bedroom,

leaving him to lock up. Her good-night kiss was correct but cool and her condition ruled out any greater intimacy even if her attitude had not. As he switched off the light, Paul remembered that he still had not told her of the scuffle with Wynne's ex-husband. Once again, this hardly seemed to be the moment for it.

"Of course, you're the head of the family and whatever you decide is what we'll do," Sibby said the next morning. She did not need to add that compliance was not the same thing as approval. She accepted because she could do little else; however, she retaliated by making it plain that it was his decision alone and he must bear the responsibility for it. Paul counted on time to ease the marital tension. Sibby, though quick to anger, was incapable of carrying a grudge long.

He stopped at police headquarters on his way to work to discuss the Fiesta parking, the chore which he had forgotten yesterday, thus leading to the sordid encounter with Fred Rossi. Orchestra Beach, although an incorporated community, had no police force of its own. For the sake of economy, it had joined several nearby communities to contract for law enforcement services with the county. Police headquarters was actually a sheriff's substation headed by a sergeant and staffed by a pair of officers and a meter maid who wrote parking tickets. Since Orchestra Beach had little crime, the arrengement worked quite satisfactorily.

Sergeant Lupo, a veteran of many past Fiestas, was already on top of the situation. Two dozen special deputies from the sheriff's reserve were being called to duty for the periods during which peak attendance was anticipated. Lupo took a dim view of the gala celebration. "Eleven and a half months of the year I got the softest touch in the world," he complained. "But the other two weeks—keyrist!" Not all of the increase in lawlessness—largely drunkenness, petty theft and other minor crimes—could be blamed on the visitors. The permanent population also found the carnival an invitation to behave in a fashion unthinkable at normal times.

"Cheer up, Sam," Paul consoled him. "If this fog doesn't lift, maybe nobody'll come."

"All the fog'll do is cause more traffic accidents. Anyway, it won't last."

Lupo was right about that; when Paul went into the bank at ten, the sun was shining brightly, a full hour earlier than on the previous morning. As he left the teller's window, George Dickman hailed him. Paul inquired about the success of his dinner party.

"Everything came out fine." George leered. "Went in even better. Say, I found that guy's card."

"What guy?"

"You know, the credit investigator. Hold on—it's in my desk."

Paul, in a hurry to get to the office, told him to forget it. He knew now that the supposed credit investigator had been Joe Chalk or another FBI agent checking on Victor Vandamm's acquaintances.

Although he was late, Wynne was even later. She arrived shortly after Paul, explaining that she had been at the garage with her Volkswagen, which was suffering from a cracked block. Wynne, depressed and listless, appeared in need of repairs herself. Later, when Tom Easley had gone to lunch and they were alone in the office, he asked if there had been trouble at the apartment following his departure.

A little, Wynne admitted. She didn't seem inclined to elaborate, so he refrained from probing. He did feel obliged to add that he stood ready to assist in any way he could—while not expecting that she would take him up on the offer, naturally.

Wynne surprised him. "There is something you could do, Paul. I really hate to ask but . . ."

"Anything within reason," he told her, leaving implicit the corollary: that he would be the judge of what was reasonable and what was not.

"I was wondering if you might give me an advance on my salary."

Paul pursed his lips. "Um. Is Rossi badgering you for dough?"

"Not in so many words. But all I've ever really been to him is a meal ticket. I thought that he might leave me alone if I could give him some money. I know what you're going to say. He'll simply spend it and come right back for more. Perhaps by then I'll have decided what to do."

"How much do you figure it would take?"

"Maybe—three hundred dollars?" She added timidly, "I'll understand if you say no. I don't have any right to ask you for anything."

Neither did he have the right, from a cold-blooded business standpoint, to loan her such a large sum. Yet he felt sorry for Wynne. And, to a slight degree, responsible, since it was he who had counseled her against running away. "Draw a check against the company and I'll sign it. But I hope you're not making a mistake. And, uh, let's keep this just between the two of us, shall we?"

Sibby might understand about the money. She might even understand about the fight. But to expect her to understand about both the fight and the money . . . well, that was asking a bit much from a wife who was already angry with him.

Newcomers to the mesa, spying the building which sat a hundred yards off the highway, frequently assumed that it was a laboratory, a school or a clinic. It was, in fact, something of each. The two-story modern structure with wings radiating from a central hub was the home of the Institute for the Study of the Behavioral Sciences.

IBS was a child of the age of cybernetics; twenty years earlier nothing like it had existed because no need had existed. Today, it was one among many similar institutions which served the new technology. Outsiders often called it a "think tank"—a term which those who worked there detested—implying that it was a refuge for eggheads and oddballs devoted to esoteric pursuits. The truth was considerably less bizarre. If asked to define its function in one word, IBS would have chosen "communication." In a computer-oriented society, as communication between machines increased, communication between men decreased. IBS's mission was to explore, define and improve human relationships: both man to man and man to himself. It worked closely with, but was not a part of, the university; its clients were drawn chiefly from the scientific and technical firms with whom they shared the mesa. IBS's discipline was a combination of psychology, sociology and theology (with a smattering of pharmacology). Thus, the starfish-shaped building contained equipment like a laboratory, housed classrooms like a school, and was staffed like a clinic.

Joe Chalk gave his name to the receptionist, who confirmed that the executive director was expecting him and directed him down the proper corridor. A man in a baggy tweed jacket came to meet him, hand outstretched. "Mr. Chalk? A pleasure. I'm Lawrence Shevlin."

He was athletic in movement, nearly as tall as Chalk

but thirty pounds lighter. His balding head made him appear older than his age, which was forty-plus. The gray-flecked Van Dyke beard and hornrim spectacles gave him the air of a Cambridge don. However, there was nothing pedantic about Shevlin's cordial manner, and his voice carried the mellow cadences of Virginia. He ushered Chalk into a comfortably appointed office and directed him to a leather chair beneath a large map of the world.

Chalk said, "By the way, Tony Aiello told me to say hello. I believe you two worked together in New York last year."

"New Jersey," Shevlin corrected. "I was a consultant on that security case at Princeton. How is Tony?"

"Still back East and hating it."

"I sympathize with him. I never thought I'd care for California myself, but after less than six months out here I'm completely hooked. Of course, in Tony's line of work a man goes where he's sent." Shevlin sat down behind his desk and eyed his visitor curiously. "Well, what does the FBI want of me this time, Mr. Chalk? I'm assuming that this isn't a social call."

"I'd like to chin with you about one of your former pupils. Victor Vandamm. I'm sure you remember him."

Shevlin grimaced. "What a shocking tragedy. Certainly, I remember Victor. I'll have to challenge the term 'pupil,' though. Victor participated in one of my encounter groups—but he wasn't actually my pupil any more than I was his teacher. The theory behind these groups is that each person teaches himself. I merely act as the catalyst." He grinned engagingly. "Do I seem to be splitting hairs? Well, what do you expect from a semanticist?"

"Put it any way you like, Doctor. You did know Vandamm pretty well, didn't you?"

"I'm not sure that anyone knew Victor well."

"I'll buy that. But you were in a position to read him better than anyone else around here. You ran a personal evaluation on him when he went to work for Keller Corp. Did anything strike you as odd?"

"Yes," Shevlin said calmly. "If by odd you mean—queer."

Chalk looked startled. "You knew Vandamm was a homosexual? Why the hell didn't you report it?"

Now it was Shevlin who registered amazement. "But I did."

"I've read your report myself, Doctor. There's not a mention of it."

Shevlin picked up his telephone. "Betty, bring me the file on Victor Vandamm." He spelled the name. "Mr. Chalk, I would scarcely omit such an important item as that, considering the sensitive nature of the job involved. I recall that I was surprised that no action was taken on the matter. However, IBS simply reports its findings. It's up to the client what he wants to do with them."

A young woman came into the office, placed a manila folder on the desk and departed. Shevlin leafed through it. "Here it is," he announced, plucking out a sheet of paper. "See for yourself. 'Latent homosexual tendencies.' "

Frowning, Chalk read the carbon copy. "I've never seen this before. How come it wasn't incorporated in the regular report?"

"Discretion, mainly. Homosexuality is a pretty serious accusation. Any number of persons may have access to our regular report form. When it comes to something like this —which can cost a man not merely his job but his reputation—IBS prefers to furnish the information only to those who really need to know it. In most cases, that's the head of the firm. You notice that our letter is addressed to Hank Keller personally."

63

"Hank Keller never got it. Somebody else grabbed it first."

Shevlin, studying his baffled expression, said, "I gather that there's been a security breach which involves Victor. I don't know if I can be of any help to you, but it goes without saying that I'll do whatever I can."

"Thanks," Chalk muttered. "But I'm afraid—" He started to rise, then hesitated and sat down again. "Maybe there is something you can do. I'd like your opinion on this."

He removed a small leather-bound book from his pocket and laid it, open, on the desk. "Vandamm's appointment calendar. We found it in his apartment. It's all we did find, actually. Most of it's pretty innocuous stuff, doctor and dentist appointments, that sort of thing. But there's one recurring entry that coincides with Vandamm's days off. As you can see, it's not a name but a drawing, a kind of picture. Tell me, Doctor, what does that look like to you?"

Shevlin examined it closely. "I'm a bit hesitant to say. My experience has taught me that one often sees what one has been conditioned to see. For example, a psychiatrist might call it a phallic symbol. An engineer might call it a polyhedron. A child, on the other hand, would probably call it a house—or houses, since there are two of them."

"Someone in my business might think it was shorthand for a name, a person or a place. Let's say I'm right. From what you know of the way Vandamm's mind worked, what kind of name might that picture stand for?"

He waited hopefully. "I'm sorry," Shevlin said finally. "I'd love to be the magician and pull the rabbit out of the hat for you. In all honesty I can't. I'm afraid that the only one who could tell you what Victor meant by those drawings is Victor himself."

"You're wrong about that. There's at least one other

person somewhere who can tell me. The trick is to find him. Much obliged for your time, Doctor. Sorry if I put a dent in your schedule."

"Not at all," Shevlin assured him. "I have a seminar—Personal Potential—at two, but they'll forgive my tardiness. At least, they always have. Here, I'll walk you out."

Several women were clustered in the lobby. They hailed Shevlin with good-natured reproaches for keeping them waiting, but readily accepted his apology. While he denied that they were his pupils, it was obvious that they considered him their teacher, and a highly admired one, with all the privileges thereof.

Only one took notice of his companion. "Why, Mr. Chalk!" Sibby exclaimed. "What are you doing here? I didn't know you were a friend of Larry's."

"A friend of a friend," Chalk replied noncommittally. "Nice seeing you again, Mrs. Towers."

On the way to his car, Chalk took out the appointment book and studied the little pictograms, the drawings which to him appeared to represent nothing so much as two crude houses with pointed roofs. He halted and stared back at the building he had just left, not at the roof, which was flat, but at the lobby, which was now empty.

"Towers," Joe Chalk said thoughtfully.

By five o'clock the expanded Fiesta edition of the *Dispatch* was on the press and ready to roll. Once again the weekly miracle had been accomplished. From the chaos of copy, heads and ads and despite the confusion of phone calls, last-minute additions and deletions, stories forgotten or misplaced, a newspaper was about to be born. Actual delivery was still a few hours off, but labor had begun. Those who had conceived it and carried it to term felt both satisfaction and an immense weariness.

Tom Easley, his work at an end, announced that he intended to embark on a three-day drunk and urged the boss to join him. "Sounds delightful," Paul admitted. "But the beauty pageant's tonight, and I'm one of the judges."

He was clearing off his desk when Clarence stuck his head into the office. He was the elder of the two printers employed by the *Dispatch,* a hollow-chested cadaverous man who claimed to be sixty and looked seventy. Perhaps more reliable was his boast of having worked for every major newspaper in the eleven western states (he did not add that each had fired him for drunkenness) and a good many of the smaller ones as well. When sober, he was as good a typographer as any; when intoxicated, he was still better than some. In either state, he was unfailingly pessimistic. "Got a problem," he announced with typical gloom. "The press won't run."

Paul went to investigate. Willy, the other printer, was standing beside the silent press with folded arms. As the junior typographer—an incongruous term, since Willy was at least fifty himself—he took orders rather than responsibility. Hence, he could view the calamity with interest but detachment.

A calamity it plainly was. A newspaper worked constantly against a deadline, with little time allotted for misfortunes. They seldom occurred, anyway: one story was easily replaced by another, pictures omitted and make-up shifted with no one the wiser. Even a malfunction of the linotype wasn't a tragedy, since there were two of them. But there was only one rotary press and its failure at the crucial moment of birth spelled disaster.

"Doesn't seem to be getting any juice," Clarence explained, adding, "I've been expecting something like this to happen for a long time."

Paul refrained from retorting that if that were true he

should have taken steps to prevent it. Instead, he ordered Wynne to telephone the manufacturer's representative and have a service man sent out immediately. While waiting, he tinkered with the press himself in the hope that it might, as machines often did, unaccountably cure its own ills. It did not.

Wynne returned, her face concerned. "Their office was closed, but I finally caught the manager at home. He says that one of their service men is sick and the other is someplace in Orange County on another emergency. The best he can promise is first thing in the morning."

Paul swore. "We can't wait that long! The paper's got to get out tonight or we're up a creek. What the hell have I got a service contract with those people for, anyway?" Yet anger solved nothing, so he turned to Clarence. "Think you and I can fix the damn thing?"

"I doubt it," Clarence said glumly. "Guess it wouldn't hurt to give it a go, though."

Willy declared himself out immediately with the excuse that it was his wife's birthday and there was a surprise party planned and if he wasn't there . . . Paul dismissed him; if two men were not sufficient to repair the balky press, three men wouldn't be, either.

Wynne volunteered to remain, but he told her to go home also, since there was nothing she could do to assist them. She bid him good night and good luck. However, when he went into the front office a few minutes later, she was still there. "I'm trying to get a taxi," she explained. "My car's in the garage."

He'd forgotten about it. "What is this—the revolt of the machines? Never mind the taxi. Those robbers'll charge you two bucks. Take the van instead."

"But what'll you do?"

"Looks like I'm stuck here. It's only a few blocks to the

auditorium and I can beg a ride home from somebody after the beauty pageant." He pressed the keys into her hand. "Just be sure to get the van back in time to deliver the paper tomorrow. That is, if there is a paper."

After Wynne departed, he telephoned Sibby. She was distressed but understanding. "Of course it's all right about dinner, darling. Try to grab a bite somewhere, promise? Yes, I'll be fine. As a matter of fact, Eileen just dropped by. Eileen Howard, you know. And since she's a widow too—Rocky's back in Chicago—I think I'll convince her to eat with me." A short off-telephone discussion ensued, which Sibby concluded with "If you don't, I'll be forced to watch television—and there's nothing decent on! Eileen is going to stay," she informed Paul, adding in a lower voice, "Are you okay, honey? I've been wondering all day if you were mad at me for the things I said."

Paul grinned at the feminine code which, translated, meant that she had gotten over her vexation. "I'm in good shape. Wish I could say the same for the press. Keep your fingers crossed, huh?"

Sibby promised to do that and pray as well. Neither her prayers nor his curses produced any immediate results. The two men sweated over the big press, stripping it down and reassembling it again, hopeful each time that they had solved the problem. Success continued to elude them. Both agreed that the difficulty lay in the machine's electrical system—but where? By the time seven-thirty rolled around, Paul realized that they were in for a long evening. Clarence also; he requested a break and slipped out, mumbling that he needed a cup of coffee. Paul watched the old man shamble across the street to The Stage Stop. The tavern did serve coffee, but he suspected that Clarence was after something stronger.

He took advantage of the respite to phone George Dickman. "Need a favor, buddy. I'm due to judge the beauty pageant at eight and I'm tied up here. How about filling in for me?"

"Anything for a friend," George replied with alacrity. "Much as it goes against my religion to watch a bunch of beautiful fillies prance around in bikinis. Say, does a judge get to examine the contestants to make sure they're not wearing falsies?"

Paul went back to work. "Maybe I've found it," he told Clarence when the printer returned, sucking on a mint which did not conceal the odor of whiskey. "I think our problem's here, in the switch box."

In this he was proved correct. However, locating the trouble and correcting it were not the same. The switch could not be repaired and a replacement at this time of night was unavailable. They eventually arrived at a stop gap remedy by cannibalizing parts from the old flatbed press used for job printing. It was nine-thirty before Paul, weary but triumphant, was able to announce, "Well, that's that." The *Dispatch* was ready to roll, five hours behind schedule but still in time to meet its publication deadline.

"Go on and beat it," he told Clarence. "You're bushed and I can handle the run myself." He was moved by more than consideration for the printer's age. Clarence had gone out for "more coffee" three times in the past two hours and his eyes were glassy, though not with fatigue. He promised to be less help than hindrance from now on. Paul viewed his weakness tolerantly; on the other hand, he saw no reason to pay Clarence time and a half to indulge it.

The press, as if to make amends for the anguish it had caused, operated splendidly on the makeshift repairs. Paul had little to do except supervise the operation. By eleven-thirty, the Fiesta edition was printed, folded, cut and stacked, ready for distribution the following morning, with nothing to indicate that there had ever been any reason to fear that it wouldn't be.

It wasn't until he entered the parking lot behind the plant—and found it empty—that Paul remembered that he had sent the van off with Wynne. He had counted on bumming a ride home with one of his fellow judges from the beauty pageant. The pageant was long since over. The streets were innocent of traffic; the heavy fog, as well as the hour, had driven Orchestra Beach to seek hearth and home.

He debated phoning Sibby. She was undoubtedly asleep by now and, though she wouldn't complain about it, still he hated to drag her from a warm bed into the damp night. Anyway, it would take her a half-hour to dress and to make the journey, a half-hour he'd be forced to wait when every weary muscle made him long to get home as rapidly as possible. For his sake as well as hers, it was more practical to hire a cab.

He headed for the taxi stand at the corner of Presidio and Coast. He stumbled on the uneven bricks of the sidewalk and for the first time wished that Orchestra Beach would replace them with less picturesque but infinitely smoother concrete.

"I am tired," he muttered wryly. "God, I'm glad this day is over!"

But it wasn't, not quite.

Sibby had left a light for him in the living room. When Paul let himself into the house, he quickly learned that more than the lamp was burning. His wife was not snug in bed as he supposed, but sitting in the wingback chair, wide awake and fully dressed as well.

"Well, hi!" he greeted her. "Gosh, honey, I didn't expect you to wait up for me."

"Didn't you?" Her voice was icy and she turned her face away to avoid his lips. "Sorry if I surprised you."

Paul regarded her, puzzled. "What's wrong?"

"Would it be too much to ask where you've been this evening?"

"You know where I've been. Working."

"Is that what you call it? You needn't bother to lie to me, Paul. You see, I telephoned the auditorium and they told me that you'd gotten George to take your place for the judging. Because you were tied up at the office, of course." She spoke with the heavy irony of a prosecuting attorney. "But when I telephoned the office, why, oddly enough, nobody was there. Nobody at all."

"I was in back with the press. I must not have heard the phone."

"Naturally! Now why didn't I think of that?"

Paul hadn't eaten since lunch, he was dog-tired and her inexplicable hostility was the last straw. "I don't know what you're driving at, but I'd appreciate it if you'd cut out the sarcasm and get it off your chest. Just where do you think I've been tonight, anyway?"

"I don't think—I know!" she replied with equal heat. "You've been sleeping with Wynne!"

The accusation was so unexpected that he laughed. It was the wrong reaction; Sibby sprang up furiously. "Don't you dare laugh at me!" she cried in a voice that shook with anger. "And don't you dare deny it, either! You're having an affair with her!"

"Damn right, I deny it! It's the most stupid—"

"I couldn't understand the way you've been acting lately. Why you've been so irritable. Why you wouldn't take the new job. Why you didn't want to have a baby!"

Tears came to her eyes, but she blinked them away. "It all makes sense now. You're in love with her, aren't you?"

"Now listen to me, Sibby," he said gently in the hope that damping his own anger would damp hers as well. "I swear to you that I am not in love with Wynne. There's absolutely nothing between us."

"I suppose you weren't shacked up with her yesterday evening, either!" She took his surprise for guilt. "Yes, Paul, I know all about your little love nest. Eileen Howard lives at Seaview, too. She saw you creeping out of that woman's apartment and wiping away her lipstick. Eileen came here tonight to warn me what was going on behind my back."

"Good old Eileen," Paul said bitterly. "Did it ever occur to you that she might be mistaken?"

"She saw you plainly. And besides, there was the van parked—"

"I mean mistaken in her assumption. Sure I was at Wynne's apartment last evening. Her car broke down and I drove her home. I told you that."

"You didn't tell me you went inside with her."

"I needed to make a phone call."

"Oh? Has the phone company removed all their booths?"

"And furthermore," Paul continued doggedly, "that wasn't lipstick I was wiping off. It was blood."

"Really? You mean she bit you? She must be very passionate."

"No, I got slugged. And not by Wynne, if that's your next question. By her ex-husband."

"Just for using the telephone?" Sibby inquired mockingly. "Oh, come on, Paul!"

"Of course not just for using the telephone. Rossi jumped to the same ridiculous conclusion that you did. He hit me before I could explain."

"Do you expect me to believe that a man would attack

you—just step right up and hit you—unless he had some very good reason?"

"Rossi's that kind of sneak."

"And what kind of sneak are you? Something that serious happens to you and you don't even bother to tell your wife about it?"

"I was going to tell you. I was, well, waiting for the right moment."

"I don't believe you. You never really intended to tell me at all. Even if you were the most innocent lamb on earth, you still wouldn't have told me. Because that's the way you are."

"What do you mean by that? When haven't I been honest with you?"

"Never—that's when! Oh, don't look so shocked. Maybe you've never actually lied to me before now, but you've never really opened up to me, either. Sure, you can be very warm and loving—up to a point. But you've always held part of yourself back. Private property. No trespassing."

"I didn't realize you felt that way," Paul said slowly. He sensed that this accusation was the most serious she had yet made, since it at least contained some truth. "Why haven't you mentioned it before?"

"I was willing to accept it—even though it hurt—because I thought the rest of what we had made up for it. But now . . ."

"I won't say you're wrong," Paul admitted. "Maybe because I was on my own for so many years before I met you, well, maybe that does make it hard for me to open up completely, as you put it. Even to you. I'm sorry if I've hurt you, Sibby."

"It doesn't matter," she said indifferently. "I don't know why I even brought it up."

"I promise I'll try to do better in the future."

"What future? Perhaps I haven't made myself clear. I'm getting out, Paul. I wouldn't be here now if I hadn't wanted to tell you to your face. You see, I at least believe in putting my cards on the table."

Up to this moment he had assumed that the quarrel—though by far the worst of their marriage—would be settled in the usual way, with kisses. He had not foreseen this conclusion. Nor could he believe she really meant it. "Aw, honey," he murmured, moving to embrace her. "This is crazy. I love you. You're my wife."

She put the chair between them. "That can be changed. And it will be, just as soon as possible. I'm going to move in with Hank and Marilyn for a few days until I can get a place of my own. It's too late tonight, but I'll be leaving first thing in the morning."

"You mean you'd actually walk out on me?"

"Put it any way you like. Though I think it's you who did the walking." She brushed past him swiftly, adding over her shoulder, "I put your pajamas in the spare room. Good night."

Stunned, Paul watched her go, heard the bedroom door close behind her. She did not slam it, but this was more ominous that if she had; anger at least held some promise of reconciliation, where contempt did not. He lingered in the hallway for a while in case she should change her mind. When it became apparent that she would not, he knocked softly and tried the knob. The door was locked.

That Sibby had felt it necessary to lock him out of their bedroom, the place that was both symbolically and actually the altar of their marriage, infuriated him like a slap in the face. For a moment, he contemplated kicking in the panel. Then he growled "To hell with it." He stalked into the guest bedroom and put a second door between them.

He was bone-weary, but though his body begged for sleep, his brain would not accommodate it. Now and then he dozed, only to start awake with pounding heart and contracting stomach. Most of the night he stared at the ceiling he could not see while he reprised the incredible again and again. He stood condemned for a crime of which he was innocent. Sure, he had been wrong in not telling her of the fight with Rossi, but that was all, and if Sibby expected him to crawl . . . He was torn between standing on his pride and swallowing it.

He arose with the first light to face a new dilemma. His shaving gear and fresh clothing were behind the locked bedroom door. Much as he needed both, Paul was reluctant to arouse Sibby in order to get them. She was seldom in a good mood this early in the morning even on the best of days, which this certainly wasn't. Not knowing what to do, he turned on the coffee and sat down at the breakfast bar to wait for it to perk.

"Oh!" said Sibby, behind him. "I didn't know you were awake." She was fully dressed, even to nylons and heels. Though she wore make-up, her face was pale and drawn.

"Couldn't sleep. Thought I'd have a cup of coffee." There was an awkward silence. He asked, to break it, "What are you doing up so early?"

"I couldn't sleep, either. And I have some packing to do."

"Look, if you really meant what you said last night . . ." He paused to give her an opportunity to recant, then went on, "There's no reason for you to leave, you know."

"I think there is."

"What I mean is, I'll go instead."

"Why should you?"

"It's more sensible, that's why. You're the wife. You should have the house, not me. God knows I wouldn't stay here alone, anyway."

"No, I've made up my mind. You can keep the house—and the car—and everything. I'll just take my clothes and a few books."

"If anyone leaves, it's going to be me, and that's that."

"It wouldn't be right. You paid for all these things and I want you to have them."

The ridiculous argument—two passengers, each insisting politely that the other should have the favored place at the rail while their ship sank beneath them—touched the match to his anger. Paul seized her by the shoulders and shook her roughly. "God damn it! Can't you get it through your thick head that the only thing around here I want is you?"

For an instant, Sibby seemed ready to strike him. Suddenly she began to cry and then they were clinging together, fingers digging into flesh that felt no pain, murmuring incoherent apologies between kisses. Until at last, purged by the emotional storm through which they had passed but still shaken by it, they could smile weakly at each other. As in most marital battles, there was neither victor nor vanquished, merely survivors.

Paul put it into words. "We were both to blame. I'll forgive you if you'll forgive me." Gazing into her moist eyes, he said solemnly, "I swear to you that there's nothing between Wynne and me except business. I am not in love with her."

"I wouldn't really blame you if you were. She's so much prettier than I am—and smarter." Her voice quavered. "And sexier, too."

"I'll be the judge of that, if you don't mind."

She hung back as he urged her toward the bedroom. "Paul, we can't. You know, I'm still . . ."

"To hell with that. It hasn't stopped us before. I need you, Sibby."

"Do you, darling?" she murmured tenderly. "Then you shall have me."

As they reached the door to their bedroom (Had it actually been locked against him? It seemed inconceivable now.), the telephone rang. "Darn!" Sibby exclaimed but went to answer it, kicking off her shoes and beginning to fumble with the zipper to her dress. "Yes, he's here," she said and thrust the receiver at Paul. "Your secretary wishes to speak to you," she told him in a voice from which all warmth had fled. "Strictly business, of course."

"For Christ's sake," he muttered. Of all people to phone him—and of all times . . . "Yes, Wynne," he snapped. "What is it?"

Her voice was barely above a whisper. "I'm sorry to bother you, Paul. Please forgive me—but I had to talk to somebody and you're the only one who . . ." She began to sob.

"Wynne, what's wrong? What's happened?"

"Maybe she needs another ride," Sibby suggested caustically.

"She's crying," Paul explained. "Wynne, get hold of yourself and tell me what this is all about."

Her answer came between sobs. "It's so—so horrible. Fred's been shot. He's dead!"

"My God!" Paul breathed and sat down on the bed.

"What is it?" asked Sibby, midway between curiosity and hostility.

"I just got back from the police station," Wynne continued in the same gasping voice. "I've been there all night, answering questions and . . . Oh, Paul, I think I'm going to crack up!"

"Wynne, you don't mean that you're the one who—"

"What? Oh, no! They don't know who did it yet."

"Will you please tell me what's going on?" Sibby demanded.

Paul covered the mouthpiece. "Her husband's been murdered."

"Murdered!" Sibby's eyes widened and her hands flew to her lips. "Oh, Paul—how horrible! Is she all right?"

"She doesn't sound too good."

"Let me talk to her." She seized the telephone. "Wynne, Paul's just told me. Where are you? I see. Is anyone with you? Well, I want you to come over here right now. No—I absolutely insist. You can't be alone at a time like this." She brushed aside Wynne's final objection. "Then call a taxi. We'll be expecting you." She hung up. "That poor woman," she murmured. "I hope you don't mind, Paul, my inviting her to come here. What else could I do?"

"Nothing, of course." Yet he doubted if many wives would have been capable of the kindness. It was a measure of Sibby's loving nature that she could instantly put jealousy aside and open her heart to one whom she considered, justifiably or not, to be her rival. "You're a wonderful person."

"Not really. All I could think about was how I'd feel if . . ." She hugged him fiercely, not in passion, which must now be postponed, but with something akin to panic. "Oh, darling, suppose it had been you instead!"

Wynne arrived a half-hour later. She had dried her tears and managed to achieve an outward composure; however, she could not keep her hands from trembling.

She was grateful for the breakfast Sibby prepared for her, although she ate little of it. She was more grateful for the emotional nourishment and this she devoured hungrily. Dependent by nature, Wynne possessed little inner strength to draw upon—and the circumstances in which she found herself would have taxed a truly self-reliant woman.

Sibby encouraged her to talk "but only if you want to." Wynne wanted to; she needed the catharsis of sharing the tragedy with a sympathetic audience. Which, Paul gathered, the police had not been. It was understandable. When an estranged husband is inexplicably murdered, the wife is the logical chief suspect. However, their suspicions had not been strong enough to charge her with the crime, although their interrogation had been sharp and lengthy.

He learned that Rossi had met his death in the Seaview parking lot rather than in the apartment above, his first assumption. Wynne had not witnessed the slaying or even been aware of it until the police aroused her.

"Fred went out about eleven-thirty," she explained. "He was going to the liquor store for another bottle. He never came back. Some other people from the apartments —the Staffords—found him a little before midnight when they came home from the movies. I don't know how long he had been lying there."

"Didn't anyone hear the shot?"

"I guess not. I took a sleeping pill and went to bed. Anyway, some kids have been setting off firecrackers the last few nights—I suppose they got them for the Fiesta—so if anyone did hear the shot, they wouldn't think much about it." She shivered. "If only I had heard it, maybe I might have been able to do something to save him."

"There's no use blaming yourself," Sibby soothed.

Wynne clutched the absolution gratefully. "The police say that Fred died almost instantly. But just the same—"

"I know exactly how you feel. I remember how I felt the other day when Paul nearly drowned. You tell yourself: Why didn't I think of this? Or why did I let him do that? It doesn't do the slightest bit of good."

"I still can't believe that it happened. It's all so—so unreal. Why should anyone want to kill Fred?"

Another question, less rhetorical than hers, was puzzling Paul. What had Rossi been doing at the apartment at that time of night? Wynne had given him reason to assume that her former husband would be leaving town. He had advanced her three hundred dollars for this very purpose. Yet the bribe had obviously not bought her freedom. On the contrary, what Wynne had said (and what she left unsaid) strongly suggested that Rossi had merely appropriated the money, the apartment and the woman as well— and that she had permitted it. Why? He kept the question to himself. Wynne's domestic arrangements were none of his business.

"We've talked enough," Sibby decided. "You need to rest. I've made up the bed in the spare room for you."

"Oh, I couldn't! I've already imposed enough."

"Nonsense. I'm certainly not going to let you go back to that apartment, not in the shape you're in. Help me convince her, Paul."

"You're staying, " Paul told her with a smile. "Boss's orders."

Wynne allowed Sibby to lead her away. At the last instant she turned back. "Oh, Paul—I nearly forgot. I'm sorry about the van."

"What about the van?" Once again he had failed to remember that he had loaned the vehicle to her. "It's still at your place, isn't it? Don't worry, I'll have somebody pick it up."

"You can't. I mean, the police impounded it. They're looking for fingerprints or something." Wynne noticed his bewilderment. "I thought I told you over the phone. Fred was going to use it to go to the liquor store. He was shot while he was getting into it."

The substation this morning was a frenzied contrast to its customary torpid state. A score of uniformed men, members of the sheriff's reserve, were crowded into the small office to receive their instructions for the Fiesta, whose opening was now only hours away. Sergeant Lupo was attempting to issue orders and answer questions simultaneously.

"Did I call it?" he greeted Paul glumly. "The damn thing hasn't even begun yet and I'm swamped already."

"I came to see about getting my van," Paul explained. "I hope you're through with it. I got papers to deliver."

"That's not my headache, thank God. Talk to the boys from headquarters. They're in charge of the Rossi case."

The "boys" turned out to be men older than Paul, a Lieutenant Guild and a Sergeant Krantz, taciturn veterans so typically police officers that they might have been stamped out of a mold. Since Orchestra Beach had no homicide division of its own, they had been assigned by the sheriff's department to conduct the murder investigation. Paul knew neither of them.

"Sure, you can have it back," Guild told him when he repeated his request. "We got no further use for it." The van had been impounded not in the hope of finding fingerprints but in case it might contain the bullet which had killed Rossi. More precisely, bullets; there had been two shots fired.

"One in the chest and one in the throat," Guild said dispassionately. "Damn good shooting. The guy knew his business."

"Oh? He was shot from a distance?" Paul had supposed otherwise.

"We figure the killer for across the street from the apartments, which would make it about fifty yards. That's not much of a reach for a rifle—but when you figure the fog . . ."

"Do you have any idea who shot him?"

"We're working on it. You got anything that might help us, Mr. Towers? You being the widow's boss—and I understand you're one of the few people around here who even knew the deceased."

"I didn't really know Rossi, Lieutenant. We only met once."

"How'd he strike you?"

"Unpleasantly." Which was certainly true as far as it went, and he saw no reason to elaborate. Wynne had apparently not told them of the scuffle and it bore no relation to the murder, anyway.

The officers did not pursue the subject. Since Rossi was a stranger in town (thus, presumably, having no local enemies) and since robbery had not been the motive, they favored the theory that the killing was the work of a psychopath. The method—the rifle, the haphazard choice of victim—resembled a series of slayings committed in Southern California over the past three years by a person whom they referred to as The Sniper for want of a better name.

However, they were not ruling out other possibilities, including that Wynne herself might be responsible. Paul scoffed at the notion. "Even if Wynne were capable of such a thing, which she isn't by any stretch of the imagination, she doesn't know one end of a rifle from the other."

"She could know somebody who does," Krantz suggested. "Wouldn't be the first time a wife and a boy friend teamed up to get rid of a husband."

"Wynne doesn't have a boy friend. For that matter, Rossi wasn't even legally her husband. By the way, I should tell you that Wynne is staying at my place for the moment. In case you have to get in touch with her again."

Guild regarded him with new interest. "You a pretty good friend of hers, Mr. Towers?"

"It was my wife's idea," Paul explained to prevent any misunderstanding. "She didn't think Wynne should be alone right now." He hesitated on the point of departure. "Maybe I should ask if your Sniper theory is meant for publication—or is it off-the-record?"

"Wish I thought it mattered. The truth is that a theory is all we do have and not one damn shred of evidence, for it or against it." Guild grimaced. "But that *is* off-the-record, if you don't mind."

The death of Fred Rossi occurred too late to be included in the special edition of the *Dispatch*. It did make the metropolitan newspapers, which gave full play to the Sniper angle. Paul did not regret being scooped. The *Dispatch* could not hope to be competitive, news-wise, with the dailies, and murder was not the sort of story that the local power structure cared to have emphasized. Some of the Fiesta committee even feared that the bad publicity ("rotten timing" was the way they put it; no one expressed any sympathy for the dead man) might cut down on attendance. Paul doubted it. The average man let little frighten him in his pursuit of pleasure; the continued use of cigarettes proved that. Murder, like lung cancer, was something that happened to other people.

The steady streams of traffic, pouring into the town from both north and south, indicated that he was right. The weather report also was encouraging. A building santana condition—that periodic reversal of the pressure pattern which brought dry desert winds sweeping across the southland—promised an end to the unseasonable fog.

Sibby phoned during the afternoon to report that the police had been to the house and had taken Wynne away with them. Why? Sibby didn't know; the officers had been polite but uncommunicative. She wondered if perhaps Wynne required the services of an attorney.

"Did they arrest her—or give you the idea that they intended to?" No, Guild and Krantz had said merely that further questioning was necessary. "In that case, we'd better not butt in. I doubt if Wynne's really under suspicion. Anyway, she knows she can call us if she needs help."

Sibby was willing to leave it at that. She felt sorry for Wynne, as she would anyone in trouble; however, having done all that could be done, she saw no reason to brood about it. "Are our plans still the same for this evening, Paul?"

"Yeah. I'll be leaving in a few minutes to help get the parade organized. You come down later and meet me at the end of the line of march. We'll grab a bite then and bum around a little, okay?"

"Sounds like fun. Sevenish?"

"That's when the parade's due to kick off. But you'd better get here a little early. The streets are filling up already."

The sun set clear for the first time in nearly a month, vindicating the weather bureau's forecast, and the evening promised to be balmy. By the time that the grand marshal's car led the way out of the parade assembly area, Coast Highway was lined with more than normal the number of spectators. The floats were larger than ever, the girls prettier, the bands louder. The Fiesta was off to a rousing start. Orchestra Beach settled down with a relieved grin to enjoy the fun and to reap the profits there-from.

As a member of the committee, Paul shared an open convertible with George Dickman, waving at the crowd and grinning at his companion's not so sotto voce comments on the young women they passed. "I feel horny as hell," George confessed happily. He had taken a drink at five o'clock "to get into the right mood" plus several subsequently to maintain it. "Thank God for the mini skirt! That's right, you gorgeous thing—lift it a little higher."

"Down, boy. That may be her husband with her."

"So what? It's open season on husbands around here. Present company not excepted. Did I tell you I solved the murder? It was you The Sniper was after, not what's-his-name. The van fooled him."

"George, you're an absolute genius! Figure out the motive, too?"

"Sure, The Sniper covets your sexy wife."

"Driver, take us to the police station. Mr. Dickman wants to make a confession."

"Go ahead and laugh. They don't call me Superdick for nothing."

"You can talk plainer than that."

The parade turned east on Bounday Street and terminated in the high school parking lot. George set off immediately to retrace the route on foot, vowing to pick up one of the pretty (and, he hoped, available) girls whose locations he had noted. Paul waited for Sibby to join him and together they watched the rest of the parade. Both agreed that it was the biggest and best yet.

"Okay, where do we go from here?" Paul asked when the passing of the Stablein Brothers Mortuary Boys Band, traditionally the final unit, signaled the end of the parade.

"There's the midway in the park, the street dance at the plaza . . . I don't suppose you wanted to see the pageant tonight, did you? Neither did I—it's always better later on. Let's just wander, shall we?"

They strolled aimlessly, hand in hand, part of the cheerful throng which overflowed the sidewalks into the streets from which vehicular traffic was barred. The air was warm, with only the slightest of breezes stirring the jacaranda and acacia trees. The multi-hued lights and the equally colorful garb of the crowd, plus the distant strains of music, created a gaudy fairyland where Fun was king and Care banished.

"Um, I feel good," Sibby declared, squeezing his arm affectionately. Her bubbling good spirits sprang from more than the carnival atmosphere. Last night's bitter breach, though still a vivid memory, was healed. Their marriage had tottered but endured, stronger and more precious than before. "I'm happy in love. How about you, darling?"

"Likewise. I'm hungry, too."

Sibby sighed. "That's a man for you. All right, husband, I'll feed you."

"Right here?"

"Food, you clown. The other will have to wait for later."

They purchased hot dogs at an outdoor refreshment stand and continued to stroll, pausing to scrutinize the sidewalk displays set up by the local artists' colony. Later, they bought coffee which they sipped seated on the steps of the library. "Feel better now, master?" she inquired.

"*Estómago lleno, corazón contento*—as we Spaniards say." His stomach was far from full, but his heart was exceedingly content. In addition to the emotions which stirred her and which he shared, Paul was warmed with the knowledge that for the first time in several weeks he had no pressing responsibilities to meet. The next edition of the *Dispatch* was seven days away and with the Fiesta officially launched, his duties in that area were over. "Finish your coffee and we'll move on."

Sibby was in no rush to quit the steps, from which vantage point she could comment upon the passing merrymakers. "Look, Paul—there's the whiskerino posse!"

A half-dozen booted young men, members of the junior chamber, strode by, tin stars on their chests and six-shooters on their hips, in search of beardless victims to hale before the kangaroo court. "Not so loud!" Paul cautioned. "They'll get me soon enough, anyway."

"Aren't a mustache and sideburns enough?"

"For me, yes. For the posse, no." The vigilantes passed without noticing him. "Hey, there's Marilyn and the kids!"

"Where? Oh! Hi, Marilyn—over here!"

Marilyn Keller was shepherding the three youngest members of her brood. "The older ones think that the Fiesta is like nowhere, man," she explained. "These don't, unfortunately, and they're nearly driving me out of my mind." However, she appeared as unflustered as usual.

"Where's Hank?"

"Working late at the plant, the coward. He did send a stand-in, though."

Once again, Paul had failed to notice Joe Chalk. Although he wore a flowered sport shirt and rust-colored slacks, the FBI agent possessed the chameleon-like ability to blend into his background. His greeting was neutral also.

"We're heading for the midway," Marilyn informed

them as her children tugged impatiently at her hands and skirt. "Want to come along and see a woman torn into three parts?"

"Love to." Sibby grabbed for her small relatives. "Come on—Aunt Sibby'll race you!"

They scampered off. Paul, Marilyn and Chalk followed more sedately. The midway was set up in Keller Park, named for Sibby's grandfather, and consisted of a small roller coaster, merry-go-round and ferris wheel, plus assorted rides which spun horizontally or vertically or both. Sibby had purchased a string of tickets as long as her arm by the time the other adults arrived and, as excited as a child herself, was arguing with the youngsters about which attraction to visit first. The issue was settled, with Marilyn accompanying her son on the roller coaster while the two little girls marched off to the ferris wheel with their aunt. Watching the affectionate way they clung to her hands—and her sure control of them—Paul reflected that perhaps, at last, it was time for Sibby to have a child of her own. Of our own, he amended.

"Go for a beer?" Chalk suggested. An open-air café stood near the entrance to the park, a welcome oasis for parents who could observe their offspring at play somewhat removed from the frenzy. Paul joined him at one of the round metal tables and a waitress eventually brought them two foam-topped steins.

"Speaking of business," Chalk said abruptly, as though changing the subject (however, Paul suspected he thought of little else), "maybe you can help me. You know, the Vandamm affair."

"How's your investigation going?"

"It isn't. I'm stymied."

"No leads to the—what'd you call it? —the KGB?"

"I got a lead, all right. Trouble is, I haven't been able

to do anything with it. Vandamm left an appointment book and I'm pretty sure that certain entries refer to his meetings with Comrade X, the agent he was working for." Anticipating the next question, Chalk shook his head. "No, it isn't a name. It's a picture, a symbol which I figure could stand for a name. Matter of fact, I had a wild idea that it might even stand for your name, Mr. Towers."

After a moment Paul laughed. "I don't know whether to be flattered or insulted. Are you serious?"

"If you think that's far-out, you should hear some of the ideas I got from Doc Shevlin out at IBS." He snorted. "Don't worry, you check out clean. By the way, I find that you hail from Nebraska. Whereabouts?"

"Prichard. It's a wide spot in the road about halfway between Omaha and Grand Island."

"I'm from Iowa myself." He continued quickly, as if regretting the personal glimpse, "Anyway, since I can't seem to tie the symbol to a person—including you—I'm wondering if maybe it stands for a place. This is where you come in. You know the area." With his finger, he drew two congruent squares on the table in beer foam, then added a pitched roof to each. "Ever seen anything like this around here?"

Paul stared at the crude picture until the dissolving foam made its outlines indistinct. "No," he said finally. "I've never seen anything like that around here. Are you sure that was how it looked?"

"Damn right I'm sure. Well, I did leave out what could be the doors—that is, if you buy the idea that it's some sort of house." Chalk grimaced. "Nothing, huh? Okay, do me a favor and keep your eyes peeled. You might just run into what I'm looking for."

Sibby returned with her nieces, out of tickets and out of

breath. "You sure have it soft," she accused the two men, "sitting here drinking beer while us women do all the work." Nevertheless, she confessed to enjoying herself hugely. "I'd forgotten how much fun these silly rides can be. Paul, come with us this time."

"I think we should be heading home, honey."

"Already? Why, it's barely nine o'clock! The night is young."

"But your husband isn't. It's been a long hard day. I didn't get much sleep last night, either."

"I'd forgotten." Sibby eyed him remorsefully, feeling that his fatigue was in large measure her fault. "Okay, darling, I'll take you home." This did not set well with the little girls nor were they placated by her promise to bring them back "another time." Experience had taught them that adult pledges of this sort were usually unredeemable. Marilyn arrived to quell their clamor with a motherly ploy: "Hush up or I'll take you home, too!" Paul and Sibby were permitted to make their escape on those terms.

As they walked toward where she had parked the Toyota, Sibby asked, "Are you all right? I know you're tired—but is something else wrong?"

"I do feel punk," he admitted. "Maybe it was that hot dog. I'm sorry to be a wet blanket and break up your fun."

"I don't mind a bit," she fibbed gallantly. "There'll be other nights. You should have said something earlier."

"I was fine earlier. It hit me all of a sudden."

"I hope you're not coming down with a summer virus. I'm going to give you a hot toddy and tuck you in the minute we get home."

"Thank you, doctor. I do like your bedside manner."

Their route led them past the plaza. The brick-paved square lay in the exact center of the business district at the point where Presidio and California Streets intersected. It had been intended to be the hub for both secular and religious authority, in true Spanish fashion; the city hall faced Our Lady of Grace Church. Actually, the real action was found on Coast Highway, where the banks, hotels and retail stores could take advantage of the flow of north-south traffic. The Fiesta had restored the plaza to its intended importance, if only fleetingly. Plywood was placed across the reflecting pool to serve as a bandstand, and a street dance was in progress. The crowd was nearly as large as that which jammed the midway and thanks to the music—dating from the forties and fifties—considerably older.

"Want to dance?" Paul asked his wife, knowing how she loved it.

Sibby wavered between temptation and concern. "I don't think you feel up to it."

"Oh, one dance won't kill me. Even if it did, what better way to go than in your arms?"

"I wish you wouldn't talk like that," she scolded. "Even as a joke. Especially after . . . No, I won't have you wearing yourself out for my sake. We'll skip it this time."

The decision was taken out of their hands by the sudden appearance of George Dickman. "So there you are!" he cried, as if he had been searching for them. "I knew you must be close at hand by the way the lights grew brighter, the breeze sweeter. Not you, fella. You."

Sibby giggled. "George, I think you're smashed."

"Barely dented, my dear." George had obviously been true to his sworn intention of staying "in the right mood." He bowed elaborately. "And this, I believe, is my dance."

"Thanks, but we're on our way home."

"You can go home with him anytime. But how often can you dance with me? Listen—they're playing our song! What is it, by the way?"

"Paul, you tell him—"

"Tell me what? That he doesn't trust you to dance with me? The nerve of the bum after he stole you right out from under my nose, too!"

He was kidding, of course. Yet not completely, as is so often the case when liquor permits hidden resentments to surface. Paul shrugged. "Better humor him, Sibby. If you don't give him a dance, he'll pout for the next year."

"Well, all right. But just one."

"That's what she says now," George chortled with a leer. "But once you're in my arms, madam . . ." He seized her and they whirled away into the swarm of dancers.

Paul watched them for a moment, thinking that they danced well together. He wondered if she might have married George had he not come along. Sibby denied the possibility ("You're the only man in the world for me, darling!"), but still . . . Life followed no preordained plan; rather, it seemed composed of a series of accidents, fortuitous and otherwise. A man's fate—if you believed in such a thing—was not determined solely by his own choice but by others as well, choices which he could neither anticipate nor control.

Engrossed in his reflections, he stared at the dancers without actually seeing them and was jostled by the passers-by without actually feeling them. A part of the crowd yet apart from it, Paul was not aware that he had been joined by another man until a voice spoke in his ear.

"Let's take a walk," the voice suggested. Paul felt something round and hard jab into his ribs. It could have been the point of a cane or a fountain pen, even a finger. Yet he knew instinctively that it was a pistol.

He turned his head sharply, more startled than afraid. "Don't make any foolish moves," the stranger cautioned. He was smaller than Paul and older, an average middle-aged man with an unmemorable face. If there was anything unusual about him, it was his clothing; he wore a brown business suit instead of the casual garb of the other Fiesta-goers. He carried the suit coat over his arm, less in deference to the weather than to conceal the weapon.

"Who are you?" Paul asked huskily. "What do you want?"

The gunman answered neither question. "Let's go." He increased the pressure of the pistol muzzle.

"Look, if it's my money you're after—"

"Start walking—unless you'd rather die right here."

"You're crazy! You wouldn't dare shoot with all these people around."

The gunman called his bluff. "The light's bad and the music's loud. I can plug you, drop the gun in that trash can and be gone before you even hit the ground. Now move!"

Paul cast a desperate glance around, seeking help and seeing none. Sibby and George were on the farthest fringe of the dancers. Neither was looking in his direction nor would they have been aware of his peril if they had been, anymore than were those who stood almost within arm's reach.

The gunman herded him toward the greater darkness of California Street. He no longer held the pistol against his captive's body where it might be knocked aside. Instead, he took up a position behind Paul and slightly to his left. Anyone watching might have concluded that the two men merely happened to be walking in the same direction.

As they neared the corner, Paul hesitated. "Aren't you even going to tell me what this is all about?"

"You know."

"Believe me, I don't. There must be some mistake—"

"Cut it out," his captor replied with a tinge of scorn. He added, "If you're thinking about jumping me, think again. I've got damn good reflexes."

He had read Paul's mind. The warning—plus his refusal to accept the incredible possibility that the gunman meant to kill him—caused him to put the half-formed intention aside. There had to be another way out of the trap, persuasion perhaps, or . . .

"Well, hey now!" cried a voice. "Look who we got here!" Turning the corner, Paul found the sidewalk blocked by a group of grinning young men in jeans and sombreros, the whiskerino posse. "We done caught ourselves a couple of live ones!" They surrounded the pair, delighted to have a member of the Fiesta committee fall into their clutches.

"What is this?" the gunman demanded and again Paul felt the jab of the hidden pistol.

"You're under arrest," the freckle-faced leader informed them with mock gruffness. "No beards—a clear-cut violation of Fiesta Ordinance Number One. Going to come along quietly?"

The gunman managed to sound tolerantly amused. "Sorry, fellows. Not tonight. We're in a hurry."

The posse looked aggrieved. The charade was contingent upon the cooperation of the victim; force was never employed. Few, however, refused to go along with the gag. Freckle Face—at the moment Paul could not remember his name—tried again. He put his hand on the butt of his six-shooter, which was loaded only with blanks, of course. "Mean to say you're resisting arrest?"

"Sorry," the gunman repeated, and this time there was an edge to his voice. "Let us by."

"It's only in fun, mister," Freckle Face chided. "Tell him, Paul."

"That's right. It's only in fun." Paul took a tentative step away from the pistol which, he felt sure, was not loaded with blanks. And when no bullet came, a second bolder step. Although the gunman was armed and the others were not, their mere presence rendered him impotent. "I surrender, men," he told his unwitting rescuers. "Do with me what you will."

"Atta boy! How about you, mister?"

The gunman seemed to be studying his options. Finding none to his liking, he commenced to sidle backward. "I don't play games." His eyes found Paul's and Paul could read their frustration. "Some other time." With that threat he turned swiftly and vanished around the corner.

"What a sorehead!" one of the posse muttered.

"Well, one out of two ain't bad," Freckle Face decided. "Okay, Paul, you got a date with the judge. Hey, what's wrong?"

"Just a little dizzy." He held onto the other man's shoulder until his legs ceased trembling. Concerned, the posse offered to call off the game and release him. Paul shook his head. "Nothing doing. I'm your prisoner and at the moment I can't think of a thing I'd rather be."

George returned to where Sibby fidgeted. "I've made the complete circle, even looked inside the church. He's nowhere to be found."

"What do you suppose could have happened to him?" Sibby fretted, midway between annoyance and apprehension.

"Say, you don't suppose he took offense, do you? I kid Paul a lot about how you used to be my girl, but I never dreamed I might be getting under his skin—"

"Oh, don't be silly. Paul's not like that at all." She grimaced. "Of course, it's not like him to go off without saying anything, either. I know he wasn't feeling well, but . . ."

"Maybe he got tired and decided to wait for you in the car. Sure, I'll bet that's where he is."

However, the Toyota was locked and empty. Nor was the missing man to be found at the *Dispatch* office, George's next suggestion. They trotted back to the plaza, thinking that he might have returned in their absence. He had not and Sibby, fully alarmed by now, said, "George, maybe there's been an accident. Do you think we should call the police?"

"There's got to be a simple explanation," he soothed. "You stay right here and let me ask a few people if they've seen him."

He was back almost immediately, grinning broadly. "What'd I tell you? The whiskerino posse picked him up and marched him off to the hoosegow."

"Oh, thank goodness!" Worry relieved, irritation returned. "But why did Paul go along with that foolishness, anyway? That's all it is, you know, a bunch of grown men acting like children!"

"Write a letter to the editor," George advised. "Who, come to think of it, happens to be your husband. Want me to go with you to rescue him?"

"Thanks, but I've already wasted enough of your evening."

He eyed her with uncharacteristic seriousness. "You can call on me for help anytime. Anytime at all, Sibby."

She understood his meaning but chose to misinterpret it. "I know that. You're Paul's best friend."

"Sure I am," he retorted, reverting to his normal flippancy. "Well, give my regards to what's-his-name."

The kangaroo court—"Judge Hangem High presiding" —had been established in a corner of the supermarket parking lot. The bar of justice consisted of wooden planks set across a pair of packing crates. The jail (labeled "hoosegow" with the s reversed) was a tiny chicken wire enclosure ruled by a ferocious-looking deputy armed with enough weapons to equip a platoon. During the rest of the year he operated a beauty parlor.

The presiding magistrate was suitably attired for his role also in a battered stovepipe hat, a rusty frockcoat and unmatched trousers. He was a retired admiral and one of Wilson Keller's closest friends; Sibby had gone through school with his daughter. "Glad you showed up," he greeted her affectionately. "I hope you came for your husband." The judge gestured at the flimsy stockade. Sibby spied Paul slouched on a bench within it. "We can't get rid of him. I passed the usual sentence—one buck or fifteen minutes in jail—and darned if he didn't choose the lockup. Couldn't talk him out of it."

The judge was concerned that Paul was setting a dangerous precedent which, if followed by others, might do the Fiesta out of considerable revenue. Most men were glad to part with the dollar in exchange for their freedom and a souvenir pardon which granted them immunity from future arrest.

Sibby paid the fine. Even then, Paul seemed oddly reluctant to leave the stockade. He had no explanation for his behavior, merely shrugging in response to her questions. Sibby was struck by his haggard appearance.

"Paul, you don't look good at all. I'm worried."

"I'm all right," he muttered unconvincingly. "Let's get out of here."

"Maybe you should wait here until I get the car—"

"No, I don't want to be alone." Yet he walked so rapidly that she had difficulty keeping up with him. He glanced over his shoulder frequently. Only when they reached the Toyota did his agitation appear to ebb. Sibby, fearing that he was seriously ill (what else could account for his behavior?), offered to drive. "I said I'm all right," he snapped. She decided it wiser not to argue the matter.

She noticed that he was not taking the direct route home. He replied shortly that he wanted to go a different way for a change—and was there anything wrong with that? They drove for a while in silence, during which he stared at the road as if oblivious to her presence.

"I've been thinking," he said suddenly. "Why don't we throw a few clothes in a suitcase and take off?"

"What?" she asked, startled. "You mean right now—in the middle of the night?"

"Yes. Just jump in the car and go. How about it?"

"But where do you want to go?"

"Anywhere. I don't care, as long as it's away from here."

"Paul, what's come over you? We can't simply pick up and leave on the spur of the moment. There's the Fiesta, for one thing. And I'm singing at church Sunday, for another."

"The Fiesta can get along without me now. And you can arrange for somebody to sub for you. Please, Sibby! I need time to sort things out, to come to some kind of decision—"

"A decision about what? Paul, you've got to tell me what's bothering you!"

He said carefully, "Call it a combination of things. I feel that I've got to have a vacation. Not tomorrow or next week, but right now. Is that too much to ask?"

"No, I suppose not." She studied him, bewildered by his urgency. But love can succor without fully understanding, and Sibby loved her husband. "Whatever you say, darling." The decision made, she commenced to warm to it. "It might be kind of exciting, at that. But what's become of the man I married, the one who always insists on planning everything to the $n$th degree?"

Her teasing drew no smile, sheepish or otherwise. He said somberly, "Some things you can't plan. You only think you can."

"That's what I've been telling you for years." Nevertheless, Sibby began some planning of her own as she tried to anticipate what the extempore excursion would require in the way of clothing and equipment. As they turned onto Cabrillo Court, she mused, "It would help if I knew what sort of weather—" She was sent lurching forward as he applied his foot unexpectedly to the brake. "Paul!"

"That car—what's it doing in our driveway?"

She recognized the sedan since she had seen it earlier that day. "Why, it's the police again! Paul, you scared the life out of me. I nearly went through the windshield."

"Sorry," he muttered. "You all right?"

"Thank God for seat belts. I do wish you'd give me some warning before you . . ." Sibby regarded the prowl car with a frown. "What do you suppose they want now? Say, maybe they've brought Wynne back."

Lieutenant Guild and Sergeant Krantz were standing on the porch; Wynne was not with them. Seeing the owners arrive, they came across the grass to meet them at curbside. "Didn't mean to block your drive," Guild apologized. "Want us to move?"

"No need. I wasn't going to put it in the garage, anyway."

Guild touched his hat brim politely in Sibby's direction. "Forgive us for bothering you at this time of night, Mrs. Towers. We have to talk to your husband for a few minutes."

Sibby refused to be dismissed, suggesting instead that

they all go inside "where it's more comfortable." The officers hesitated and accepted. However, they declined her offer of coffee; this was plainly not a social visit. They perched on the living room sofa, not quite relaxed but not ill-at-ease either, and allowed their hostess to make conversation with only token assistance.

"Well, gentlemen, what'd you have in mind?" Paul asked when Sibby paused.

Krantz deferred to his superior, who cleared his throat. "We've had another chat with Mrs. Rossi—"

"How is she?" Sibby interrupted.

"Fine," Guild replied briefly. He waited to see if Sibby meant to pursue the subject, then continued, "She's added a few things to the story she told us previously, Mr. Towers—things we'd like to discuss with you. First, she admits that she's in love with you and that her husband knew it. Second, she tells us that you and Rossi fought over her at the apartment the night before the murder. Third—"

"Hold on," Paul said. "I think you're misinterpreting what Wynne told you. Maybe she's in love with me and maybe she isn't. I'd call it more of a crush on the boss, if that. Anyway, I haven't done anything to encourage her."

"Paul and I have discussed it," Sibby said helpfully. "A crush is exactly what it is, nothing more."

Guild nodded. "But you did have a fight with Rossi over her, didn't you?"

"Not exactly. What actually happened was that I drove Wynne home after work—her car broke down—and stopped in to use the phone. Rossi was there. He jumped to the wrong conclusion and threw a punch before I could explain."

Krantz asked, "Why didn't you mention it to us this morning?"

"Maybe I should have. I didn't consider it relevant."

"Let us be the judge of what's relevant and what isn't," Guild suggested. "What'd Rossi do after you explained the situation—apologize?"

"He wasn't the type to apologize. But I do believe he knew he'd made a mistake."

"He didn't threaten to cause trouble for you?"

"Certainly not. What trouble could he cause for me?"

"Then why did you give Mrs. Rossi three hundred dollars to get him out of town?" Guild took note of Sibby's gasp. "I guess that's something your husband didn't discuss with you, Mrs. Towers."

Paul said angrily, "I don't know who's coloring the story, you or Wynne, but I don't appreciate the insinuation. I didn't 'give' Wynne anything. She asked me for an advance on her salary and I agreed out of friendship. What she did with the money was her own business."

"You mean you didn't know it was intended to buy Rossi off?"

"Wynne indicated she might use it for that. Frankly, I thought it was a mistake and told her so. Rossi was the kind who'd bleed you to death and still come back for more."

"Then what did you advise instead?"

"I didn't advise anything. What are you driving at, anyway?"

Guild pursed his heavy lips. "I'll lay it out for you. Here we've got a professional blackmailer—"

"I didn't know that."

"We've checked Rossi's record," Krantz put in. "Three previous arrests for attempted extortion, one conviction. He did a couple years' time."

"Anyway, here we've got a professional blackmailer," Guild repeated, "in the kind of setup he liked. You may not know this, Mr. Towers, but Rossi did threaten to make trouble for you. The widow admits it. And you were right about him—Rossi wasn't the sort who'd take a little when he thought he could get a lot. He'd bleed you to death, I think that's the way you put it. Except that this time it was Rossi who did the bleeding."

Sibby said incredulously, "You're not actually suggesting that Paul had something to do with it, are you?"

"I'm not suggesting anything, Mrs. Towers. But blackmail is a motive."

Paul laughed. "Oh, come off it! Rossi wasn't blackmailing me and I didn't kill him."

"Of course he didn't!" Sibby flared. "Of all the ridiculous—"

"Just investigating every angle. Mind telling us where you were at the time of the murder? That would be, say, around eleven-thirty."

"I was at my office, running off the Fiesta edition on the *Dispatch*. I didn't leave there until close to midnight."

"The cabbie's log shows he picked you up at eleven-fifty. And not at your office, either."

"That's right. There wasn't any cab at the usual stand so I kept walking until I found one."

"At the corner of Junipero Street and Coast Highway—which happens to be closer to Mrs. Rossi's apartment than to your office." Guild's gaze was bland but unwavering. "Your pressman claims it shouldn't take more than an hour and a half to run off the newspaper. Since you started at nine-thirty, according to him, you could have been finished as early as eleven. Which would give you time to walk to the apartment, shoot Rossi and still be back at Junipero and Coast by eleven-fifty."

Sibby jumped to her feet, flushed with indignation. "I've heard enough of this garbage! I think you'd better leave."

"I'm not saying it did happen that way. I'm just saying it could have."

"Don't try to double-talk me, if you please! You're practically accusing Paul of murder!"

"Now let's not get excited, honey," Paul cautioned.

"I'll get excited if I want to! The nerve of them, barging in here and badgering you like this—"

The two officers rose also. "Our job is to ask questions, Mrs. Towers," Guild said patiently. "Sorry if we've upset you."

"Your job is to catch the murderer!" Sibby snapped, not at all mollified. "Find The Sniper—or whatever it was the papers called him—and leave my husband alone."

Guild seemed more amused than rebuked. "Oh, we'll catch The Sniper eventually. This wasn't his work, though. The autopsy turned up one of the bullets that killed Rossi. Wasn't a rifle, after all. It was a high-powered target pistol, foreign make, Czech we think." He eyed Paul. "You going to say something, Mr. Towers?"

"No," Paul muttered. "A pistol, huh?"

"Yep. And that doesn't fit The Sniper's pattern. I don't want you to be alarmed, Mr. Towers. I got no doubt that your story will check out in all particulars. But in the meantime I'd appreciate it if you'll keep yourself available in case we need to talk to you again. In other words—"

"Don't leave town. Is that what you mean, Lieutenant?"

"Yeah," Guild agreed with a smile. "That's what I mean, all right."

As the door closed behind the policemen, Sibby gave vent to her anger by kicking the hassock across the living room. "Those rotten bastards!" she cried, she who seldom swore at any provocation. "Is this what we pay our taxes for? So they can persecute innocent citizens? I swear that

I'm going to start phoning all of Daddy's friends the first thing in the morning. I won't rest until I pay them back for—"

"Cool it," Paul told her. "Getting mad isn't going to help."

"How can you be so calm? Don't you understand what they were insinuating?"

"I'd probably think the same thing in their place. Here's a guy who may be having an affair with his attractive secretary, who apparently pays hush money to the secretary's husband and then when the husband won't stay hushed . . ." He sighed. "Wouldn't be the first time that blackmail ended in murder. It's damn ironic that I happen to be innocent."

"Why ironic? I can think of better words than that."

"What I meant was the timing. Just when I believed that we could get away from here . . . But you heard what the lieutenant said. Don't leave town."

"Oh, our vacation." She had nearly forgotten. Nor was she really concerned that the impromptu trip must now be abandoned; if anything, she was relieved since she hadn't been enthusiastic about it, anyway. For his sake she said, "I'm sorry, Paul. I know you really wanted to go. I hope you're not too disappointed."

"It's probably for the best," he said, dismissing the matter with a shrug in odd contrast to his previous agitation. "It was tempting to believe that I could solve my problem by running away from it. Never works. I'll just have to face it instead."

"What problem, darling?" Sibby put her arms around his waist. "If something's bugging you, I want to share it with you. That's what marriage is all about, isn't it?"

"Oh," he said vaguely, "I've got to make a decision. About the future."

"It's the job, isn't it? The one Hank offered you? Listen to me, dearest. I know I gave you a rough time about it . . . but I'm behind you one hundred per cent in any decision you make. I love you, Paul."

"And I love you. I want you to remember that. Whatever the future holds, I love you more than anything in the world."

"Then everything's fine! You don't have anything to worry about. Now repeat after me: I—don't—have—anything—to—worry—about."

"I don't have anything to worry about," he said slowly. "But if—"

"No buts." Sibby pulled his mouth down to hers. After a while, she sighed contentedly. "See how simple it all is when you obey me?"

They kissed again and then, with unspoken mutual consent, began to move toward the bedroom, still holding each other tightly. They spoke no more except to murmur endearments. Yet Sibby noted a strangely desperate quality to his lovemaking, almost as if he fancied it was the last time he would possess her. Ascribing it to tension, she urged him to climax quickly, taking his satisfaction for her own. "I'm so happy," she told him afterward, and was. She drifted away into blissful nothingness, relishing the remembrance of his flesh warm against hers.

Some time later—an hour or an eternity—she imagined she felt Paul leave the bed. In the deepness of her fatigue, she could not be sure . . . and she decided that she was dreaming.

The Outrigger Motel was Orchestra Beach's newest and largest hostelry, built on the site of the original pier and occupying several additional acres of choice beachfront besides. The architecture and décor hewed to the theme of the Polynesian islands—and the prices would have gone a long way toward a down payment on one of them. Nevertheless, The Outrigger operated to near-capacity the year round and room space during the Fiesta was often booked months in advance. Even parking was at a premium both on the lush grounds and in the private boat marina. Tonight, as usual, the No Vacancy sign burned brightly. However, Paul was not seeking lodging.

Joe Chalk answered his knock alertly. The phone call had routed him out of bed, but now he was fully awake and dressed. Chalk did not observe normal business hours; Paul noted that he had even shaved.

Chalk shrugged off his apology as if a visitor at two o'clock in the morning was a routine occurrence. But neither was he inclined to waste time on amenities. As soon as the door was closed, he said, "You claimed it was important. Let's have it."

"You alone?" A glance around the room—rather small, considering the tariff—made Chalk's nod unnecessary. "This has got to be between you and me. I don't even want Sibby to know. I had to wait until she was sound asleep before I could sneak out of the house."

"Sounds serious."

Paul managed a smile. "You could call it a matter of life and death, I guess."

"Whose life?"

"Mine. Somebody's trying to kill me." He read the skepticism in the other man's eyes. "No, I'm not drunk. I'm not crazy, either."

Chalk reserved judgment on both counts. He sat down and motioned Paul to do the same. "Somebody's trying to kill you? Tell me more—like who and why."

"I'd rather start with how, if you don't mind. Four days

ago I nearly drowned scuba diving. My air tanks were sabotaged. You may remember we talked about it at Hank's the next night."

"I remember. I also remember that you called it an accident."

"That's what I thought. Actually, it was the first attempt to kill me. The second attempt was two days later, but that time they didn't try to make it look like an accident. They used a pistol. Lucky for me, they shot the wrong man. Have you read about the Rossi murder?"

"He the chap that was gunned down outside his apartment? Yeah, I read about it. I don't see the connection."

"Neither did I, not until tonight. Now it's pretty damn clear. Rossi was shot from a distance—on a foggy night—while getting into a car. That's the story that was in the papers and it's accurate up to a point. What the story didn't mention is that Rossi looked a lot like me—same height, build, hair color—and that it was my car he was getting into."

Chalk raised his eyebrows. "How come?"

"Rossi's wife is my secretary. I loaned her the van when her Volks broke down. I figure the gunman was looking for me. I was supposed to be judging the beauty contest that night, but I got tied up at the plant and canceled out. So when I didn't show at the auditorium, the gunman started searching. Maybe he came by the newspaper, but I was in back and the office was dark. I wasn't at home, either, so he checked Wynne's apartment . . . and there was the van parked at the foot of the stairs. He may have followed me there the day before when I drove her home after work. Probably figured that Wynne and I were having an affair." Paul grimaced. "He's not the only one who made that mistake. So he waited, expecting that I'd come sneaking out eventually. Rossi came out instead, a man who resembled me—at least on a foggy night—and started to get into my van. Bang! Bang!"

After a moment, Chalk grunted. "No sale, Mr. Towers. The first time could have been an accident and the second time just a coincidence. I'd say you're letting your imagination run away with you."

"God, I wish you were right! I haven't told you about the third attempt yet. Tonight, a few minutes after I left you at the park, a man stuck a gun in my back and tried to kidnap me. That wasn't an accident. It wasn't a coincidence, either. If the whiskerino posse hadn't come along—"

"Wait a minute. Are you claiming that somebody tried to put the snatch on you in the middle of Orchestra Beach —in front of a whole townful of witnesses?"

"Sure, it sounds incredible. But it happened. Anyway, you know what a crowd is like, nobody paying attention to anybody else."

"Uh-huh," Chalk said, plainly unconvinced. "How come you're telling this to me instead of going to the police? Homicide—attempted or otherwise—is their jurisdiction, not the FBI's."

"Several reasons. First, I've got no proof. The cops would put me down for some kind of nut—the same way you have. Or maybe even worse, since they're already working on the ridiculous theory that I'm the one who shot Rossi. But second, and more important, this thing is too big for the local authorities to handle."

Chalk smiled pityingly. "Don't tell me. It's a plot to blow up the world. Frankly, Mr. Towers, I don't believe you need me or the police, either. What you need is a good psychiatrist."

"What I need is help, the kind of help that only Division Five can give me."

Chalk's smile faded; his face became as expressionless as the wall behind it. "Division Five? What's that?"

"Let's not play games," Paul begged. "I know that Division Five is the hush-hush section of the FBI that handles counter-espionage. And you certainly know what Division Five is because you're one of its top field supervisors."

Chalk neither confirmed nor denied the assertion. His eyes fixed on Paul's face, he murmured, "Keep talking."

"I want to make a deal. Your help in exchange for mine. Interested?"

"I'm always interested in listening to a proposition. Even a one-sided one. I can see where I might be able to help you, all right—but damned if I can see where you might be able to help me."

"Don't knock it till you've tried it. Tonight you mentioned an appointment book, the one you found in Victor Vandamm's apartment. Could I see it?"

Chalk hesitated, then got to his feet with a shrug. "Why not?" He kept the leather-bound book in the inside pocket of his coat. He stood guard beside his visitor's shoulder while Paul studied the symbols which he had described earlier. At last he suggested, "See anything you didn't see before?"

"No." Paul raised his head with a sigh. "I still had a hope—just a tiny bit of hope—that I was wrong. But I'm not. God, I never expected to see it again!"

"Okay, okay," Chalk said impatiently. "Spill it and make it snappy. What do those houses stand for?"

"What makes you think they're houses?"

"Because they look like houses, that's why! You aren't

going to hand me some crap about polyhedrons or phallic symbols like Doc Shevlin, are you?"

"I'm surprised that a boy from Iowa didn't recognize them immediately for what they really are. You must have been away from home a long time not to know barns when you see them." He eyed Chalk expectantly. "Barns," he repeated.

"I heard you the first time. Barns, houses—what's the difference?"

"You mean Division Five never heard of Bob Barnes?"

"Who the hell is Bob Barnes?"

"It's a name that used to belong—I guess Vandamm's appointment book proves that it still does—to one of the top men in the First Chief Directorate of the KGB." Paul smiled faintly. "I don't mean the radio station down in San Diego. I mean the Komitet Gosudarstvennoi Bezopasnosti, the state security committee of the Soviet Union."

Chalk took a step backward as if the foreign phrase, sliding so easily from Paul's tongue, had made them enemies. "Strikes me you know a hell of a lot for a hick newspaper publisher. Division Five, Bob Barnes, the KGB . . . You'd better have a damn good explanation, Mr. Towers."

"I have." Paul closed his eyes as if not wishing to witness his confession. "I wasn't always a hick newspaper publisher. I wasn't always Mr. Towers, either. Once upon a time, I worked for Bob Barnes—and my name then was Eddie Young."

# EDDIE REVISITED

His name wasn't actually Eddie Young, either. Originally it had been Pyotr Avanasov, the only child of Mikhail and Anna Avanasov. Mikhail Avanasov was an officer in the Red Army ("Red" was officially dropped from the title in 1946 but was still in common usage twenty years later), a colonel of artillery and a member of the Party. Pyotr possessed no real remembrance of his father. He existed only as a smiling face in a photograph; later, even this was lost. Pyotr remembered his mother somewhat better. All mothers are beautiful to their small children. In Anna Avanasov's case the illusion was justified. She had performed with the Bolshoi Ballet before her marriage and subsequent tragedy never quite succeeded in eradicating her fragile loveliness or in robbing her of the dancer's grace.

Pyotr was born in July, 1941, the summer Hitler sent his Wehrmacht plunging deep into the Russian heartland. The war, like his father, was merely something of which he was told later. Anna and her son rode out the storm in a snug sanctuary beyond the Urals. His first memory was of Moscow, to which they returned following the Nazi capitulation. Not as a city, of course (what four-year-old can comprehend a city?), but as a sunny kingdom filled with love and laughter. Mikhail Avanasov was seldom a resident of that kingdom, his duties calling him elsewhere, yet the boy understood that he was still its king and the source of power and privilege.

When Pyotr was seven, the kingdom came crashing down. Mikhail Avanasov was a protégé of Zhdanov, hero of the defense of Leningrad and first in the Politburo pecking order. Zhdanov was widely regarded as Stalin's heir apparent—but not, obviously, by the old despot, who considered death his chief enemy and those who stood to profit from his only slightly less. In 1948, Zhdanov fell out of favor and shortly afterward died under circumstances which are still to be satisfactorily explained. His coterie fell with him. Colonel Avanasov was arrested, tried secretly and convicted of unspecified crimes against the state. He vanished into the vast limbo that is the Soviet prison system.

Since Mikhail Avanasov's only crime was guilt by association, this guilt was extended to his family. Their sentence was in some ways more devastating than prison. They were permitted to exist but not precisely to live, required to work but forbidden to prosper. Their pleasant villa in the suburbs was requisitioned; their home became one room shared with others of similar status. Anna found what employment was open to her, scrubbing the floors of the Moscow subway and sweeping the streets above it. Pyotr, though too young to labor, was not too young to punish. He was expelled from the school which had been intended to train him for future leadership. He was placed instead in an institute where he might learn to operate a machine. Shunned by former friends and play-mates who feared they might become infected with the same dread disease, subject to harassment and petty perse-cutions, mother and son became—in the jargon of the day —"un-persons."

Then in 1953, Stalin died (mortal, after all; there were many who could scarcely believe it) and Pyotr's world turned upside down once more. As successors fought for Stalin's mantle, they sought to destroy his legend. Rehabil-itation of his enemies began, quietly at first, then openly. It came too late for Mikhail Avanasov. Death had granted him a prior pardon (whether by torture, disease or a bul-let, Pyotr never learned). Rehabilitation came too late for Anna Avanasov also. Her frail body, weakened by malnu-trition and that even greater killer, hopelessness, was dealt the *coup de grâce* by tuberculosis. Rehabilitation did not come too late for Pyotr Avanasov, however.

Or did it? The bleak years between the ages of seven and twelve, said to be among the most formative of life, left an indelible impression on him. Not physically; his body survived the ordeal with the amazing resilience of the child. But his mind was irrevocably shaped by it. Hav-ing been punished by a whim of the state for a crime he had not committed—and which, by another whim, turned out not to be a crime at all—he could not render the state the unquestioning allegiance it expected. What his con-temporaries accepted as a matter of fact, he doubted as a matter of course. When they spoke fervently of "Mother Russia," Pyotr Avanasov thought bitterly of his own.

Experience had taught him cunning as well as skepti-cism. He was careful to keep his heresy hidden. The state revised its plans for his future and provided him schooling more consistent with his ability. Though far behind his classmates initially, Pyotr soon outstripped them. He possessed a superior mind and—since his credo was to survive on the best possible terms—the desire to employ it to the fullest. The academy reports rated him "outstanding dedication . . . creative intelligence . . . exceptionally gifted in languages . . . high leadership potential." Pyotr cultivated his personality also; he was as popular with his peers as with his instructors.

He had a flair for dramatics and nourished an ambition to enter the theater, a legacy from his childhood when he had shut out harsh reality by creating a more endurable world in his imagination. The state had its own ambition for him—though not as far removed from his own as it first appeared. When the time came for him to enter military service, Pyotr was posted instead to the Komitet Gosudarstvennoi Bezopasnosti. True to his credo, he accepted the assignment cheerfully and kept his reservations to himself.

The KGB—the name given to the Russian state security committee following its reorganization in 1954—employs approximately one million men and women, both inside and outside the Soviet Union. It is equivalent not only to the United States' CIA and FBI but to the National Security Agency, the Secret Service, the Immigration & Naturalization Service and the Bureau of Customs as well. Of the KGB's six active sections, or chief directorates, only the First is primarily engaged in foreign espionage. Other security functions—from counter-intelligence within the Soviet armed forces to supervision of the border guards and embezzlement and theft of government property—are divided among the remaining five chief directorates, each headed by an intelligence officer of the rank of major general or above under the overall command of a civilian member of the council of ministers.

Pyotr was placed with the Eighth Chief Directorate

(the Fourth, Fifth and Sixth Directorates do not presently exist) and assigned to the American desk because of his exceptional command of English. In this capacity, he was required to analyze U.S. government communications, read and summarize U.S. newspapers and magazines and monitor U.S. radio broadcasts. Most of his fellow workers complained of the tedium; Pyotr did not. He had only a sketchy and largely inaccurate picture of the Soviet Union's powerful rival. As he pursued his duties, another —and surprisingly attractive—image began to emerge. The more he learned, the more he wished to learn.

His diligence was marked but not understood. A year later, he was transferred to the First Chief Directorate, American Section. The change was more than one of numbers. The First, from which the agents who would serve abroad were selected, was an élite corps which stressed initiative and placed less value on conformity. Its standards were high, its training rigorous. Few men found the rewards (quite possibly including death) attractive; those who did were usually motivated by the excitement it promised. Pyotr sensed that it contained something more: the chance to find, even temporarily, a kind of freedom he had only dreamed of. He threw himself into this new job with all the dedication he could muster. He graduated at the top of his class . . . and was given his reward.

In July, 1963, a few days short of his twenty-second birthday, he was posted to Middletown.

Middletown cannot be found on any map of Russia. At that time, its existence was a closely guarded secret. A high-placed defector brought the first word of it to Western intelligence in the late sixties, and satellite photos confirmed his story. Even within the KGB itself, there were many who had never heard of Middletown and of those who had, only a handful understood its purpose. Anyone foolish enough to scale the high fence that surrounded it and fortunate enough to elude the guards would have been hard-put to decide exactly what he had discovered. A model community? A military base? A university?

Middletown was all of these, and more. It had no immediate neighbors; the closest center of population was Moscow, two hundred kilometers to the northwest. The five thousand acres which comprised it lay well off the main avenues of commerce and transportation. The plain on which it stood had been cleared of inhabitants and the air space above it restricted. (An off-course Aeroflot transport had crashlanded behind the fence in 1961 with no survivors; however, there were rumors that not all of the deaths were accidental.) The fence had first been erected to contain the shattered remnants of the German Sixth Army following the surrender at Stalingrad. Since fences of this sort—like taxes—are more readily placed than removed, it remained long after there was any real use for it . . . until the KGB found one. Within it, they built a city.

A Russian citizen would have thought the new community unlike any with which he was familiar. A citizen of the United States, on the other hand, would have considered it familiar indeed. Middletown was ingeniously devised to simulate, in microcosm, a typical midwestern American city. The KGB, with the infinite attention to detail for which it was noted, overlooked nothing to create and maintain the illusion. Middletown was run by a city government headed by a mayor and council; it had its own police and fire departments and other municipal agencies. The residents read the *Middletown Republican*, a composite of several U.S. newspapers (the "news" was always several days late but, cut off from the outside world, no one knew the difference). They listened to

WRW and watched tapes of popular American programs on Channel 4. They worked at a variety of jobs, both white collar and blue collar, and spent their wages on American brand names at the A & P, Sears, Rexall Drugs and smaller establishments. They bowled at Westside Lanes and picnicked in Eastlake Park. The marquee of the Fox Theater carried the names of John Wayne and Elizabeth Taylor and Walt Disney. The more affluent drove their own automobiles; the majority commuted by bus (an earlier streetcar line had been replaced). All this for but a single purpose, to train the men and women of the First Chief Directorate for duty within their nation's prime intelligence target, the United States of America.

In one respect only was the counterfeit city strikingly different from its real life models: There were no children. Middletown's population was exclusively adult and largely between the ages of twenty and thirty. Anyone older was usually "permanent party"—the caretaker group which operated the city—or an instructor. All had served in the United States; some had been born there.

Following a short but intensive indoctrination, Pyotr was absorbed into the mainstream of Middletown's life. Not as Pyotr but as a new identity which he helped construct and whose history he was required to memorize. Pyotr Avanasov, Russian, vanished. In his place stood Edward T. Young, American. He was given a minor executive position with Campbell Aerospace, the city's principal employer (which thriftily manufactured components for the Soviet Union's own space program), a furnished apartment . . . and a wife with which to share it.

No actual marriage ceremony was performed nor was there any courtship. Couples were paired by computer and the method worked as satisfactorily as free choice might have. The women were also First Chief Directorate trainees, although few of them were intended for overseas assignments. The KGB reasoned coldbloodedly that since marriage was the American norm, a community of single young men and women was impractical for their purpose. Furthermore, the male tensions springing from a denial of sexual relations over a long period of time—the minimum stay at Middletown was one year—would impair efficiency or lead to homosexual attachments. Thus, the "marriages" in which passion was acceptable but love was not; a number of trainees of both sexes (but, rather surprisingly, more men than women) were washed out for becoming emotionally involved with their spouses.

Pyotr—rather, Eddie—had no difficulty maintaining the expected relationship. He grew extremely fond of Alice, but the insularity bred by childhood prevented anything stronger. After an initial awkwardness, he adapted easily to his role and was as successful at it as most genuine husbands. Alice was a more than satisfactory wife, a vivacious companion and a willing bed partner. She too seemed content to play the game by its rules, although later he learned otherwise.

For Eddie, life at Middletown was exciting not only for its newness but for its freedom. The trainees were under constant observation and evaluation but he could never be certain who the observers were and he soon forgot about them. Now and then he would hear that someone had "left" (i.e., been dismissed for some offense; lapsing from English into the native tongue was the most common). Less serious infractions were punished by extending the training period. Eddie was one of the few who received no demerits. The game—as he thought of it then—appealed to his love of make believe. In time Eddie Young became quite as real to him as Pyotr Avanasov had been.

During the day he worked at the plant where his executive ability won him a promotion and a pay raise. Evenings he attended classes at the university in U.S. history and geography, customs and culture, language and slang. His favorite subject, naturally, was drama, which the university stressed. Not formal theatricals with memorized lines, but *commedia dell' arte;* the actors were thrust into a sketchily outlined situation and expected to improvise. The instructor was Bob Barnes, a witty and charming older man who—it was rumored—was one of the KGB's best operatives. Barnes preached the "inner motivation" technique of acting originated by the Russian Stanislavsky and later popularized in the United States as The Method.

"It's not enough to play a role," he told his student repeatedly. "You must live it. Not until it's second nature—until it's your only nature. Disguises won't do it. Your mind is what matters. What makes a clown? Greasepaint and baggy trousers? Hell, no! A man becomes a clown by thinking funny." And he would delight them by transforming himself, without benefit of costume or make-up, into any character they suggested, from an old man to a young girl. Doctor, soldier, laborer, child . . . Barnes captured the essence of each with ease. Eddie found him irresistible.

He was happy at Middletown, happier than at any other time in his life. He would have gladly stayed on indefinitely, but no one remained permanently, not even veterans like Barnes, and particularly not a young man who demonstrated the potential of Eddie Young. The year of training came to an end and with it his "draft notice," summoning him to a world where the make believe was practiced, not in sport, but in deadly earnest.

Middletown had transformed Pyotr Avanasov into Eddie Young; Eddie Young he remained. An airplane bore him to Czechoslovakia, a second carried him over the top of the world to Cuba, a third deposited him in Mexico City. A month after leaving Middletown, Eddie walked boldly across the international bridge at El Paso, Texas, equipped with bonafides which would have withstood the closest scrutiny had anyone bothered to examine them. No one did.

He met a man named Leigh in El Paso who furnished him a bus ticket to Chicago and an address in that city. The address belonged to a small publishing house which specialized in technical and scientific books. Behind that respectable façade, Nordstrom and Whited conducted another sort of business as a clearing house for information gathered by the KGB apparatus. Eddie expected that he would be given an espionage mission. To his surprise, he was employed by the firm in a legitimate position, that of publisher's representative.

"Is that all?" he asked.

"That's all," was the bland reply given by the man who hired him, a Mr. Cain (if there was a Nordstrom or a Whited connected with the company, Eddie never met them). "Oh, we'd appreciate it if you'd sell a lot of books, naturally."

His territory was the six southern states of Mississippi, Alabama, Georgia, Florida and the two Carolinas. His duties consisted of making the rounds of bookstores in the principal cities and promoting Nordstrom and Whited's list to the colleges and universities. His firm, though small, enjoyed a good reputation among the scientific community and published many of its doctoral theses and dissertations. Since it was his nature to do so, he made friends easily and everywhere.

At first he lived in a state of suppressed apprehension. As it became apparent he had no reason to fear detection, he began to enjoy himself. He obtained a driver's license, registered with the draft (but was never called) and filed an income tax return. He accumulated a number of credit cards and the monthly bills that went with them. He became a fair poker player, developed an interest in football and a taste for southern cooking. The man from Moscow had become as typically American as the natives with whom he rubbed elbows.

Now and then he thought of the past. Yet when he did so, it was Middletown he remembered—as if his life had truly begun there with the creation of Eddie Young. When he spoke of "back home" as most Americans did, Eddie recalled rowing in Eastlake Park, the elm trees shading University Avenue, and the grandfather clock in the window of Klein's Jewelry Store. Alice was a more wistful memory. He had not actually loved her. He had been fond of her, however, and under different circumstances would have been content with her—or someone like her—for his wife. But marriage for a man in his position was out of the question, although several young women (at least one in every large city he visited) assumed otherwise.

Now and then also, he thought of the future. He could not imagine what his superiors had planned for him. Since life was pleasant, he was in no hurry to find out. As the weeks stretched into months and the months became a year, Eddie began to dare hope that the KGB had forgotten his existence. But, of course, the KGB had not.

In November, 1965, Nordstrom and Whited instructed their southern field representative to meet with a Professor Watters to discuss publication of a text on parapsychology which the professor had written. Eddie went to the appointment blithely since such assignments were routine . . . and was stunned to discover that Watters was, in fact, his former mentor, Bob Barnes. To Eddie, the reunion was less than joyful. Barnes was a painful reminder of reality.

Barnes, however, was thoroughly pleased at meeting his protégé. "I've been keeping an eye on you," he informed Eddie. He had arrived in the United States—his third tour of duty—shortly after Eddie himself and held a high-ranking position in the apparatus. "You've handled yourself splendidly. But I expect you're anxious to get down to your real job."

"I'm ready when you are, Bob," Eddie lied. "Sorry—I shouldn't call you that, should I?"

"For tonight, it doesn't matter. I was sorry to have to bury old Bob. Maybe I'll resurrect him someday."

He had continued to pursue his avocation of painting. He showed Eddie his most recent canvases. "In memory of the dear departed," he explained, pointing out the small pictogram in the corner of each resembling two crude houses. "They're barns, of course. My private joke. You're the first person I've shared it with. Which should be some indication of my high regard for you."

As before, Eddie found himself warming to Barnes' personality. In his charming presence, it was possible to forget temporarily that he represented a force that was far from charming—and which demanded Eddie Young's allegiance and, if necessary, his life. The apparatus intended to employ him as a courier. For that reason, it had taken pains to establish him in a job where constant travel was the norm and, thus, would draw scant suspicion. Now he was being "promoted" from an area representative for Nordstrom and Whited to representative-at-large. In that capacity, he would be able to move freely around the United States and outside it as well.

Barnes divined his dismay but misinterpreted its cause.

"I know. You were looking forward to more exciting duty. Consider it a steppingstone to better things. One of these days I expect you'll be standing in my shoes, Eddie."

"I doubt if I could handle your job."

"Baloney! You've got everything it takes and more. Including the one priceless quality that can't be taught. I mean the ability—no, make that the instinct—to survive."

Eddie did not dispute the compliment. Neither did he confess that mere survival was no longer enough for him. He now wanted to survive on his own terms. Those terms were, quite simply, as a free man. The thorough indoctrination had done more than prepare him to be an American. Ironically, it had prepared him to cease being a Russian. It was not entirely accurate to argue that he had come to love this new country better than the old; he would have felt much the same in Australia or India or Argentina. He had become, in his own private conscience, a citizen of Earth rather than any one small segment of it. To be called back to serve a narrow national interest against another equally narrow was intolerable.

But what choice did he have? His service did not accept resignations. It had been impressed upon the KGB trainees what happened to defectors. They were assassinated (like Krivitsky) or compelled to spend the remainder of their lives as hunted animals (like Gouzenko). For that matter, Eddie could see no advantage, moral or physical, in exchanging one side for the other. He had learned that there was little fundamental difference between the Russian people and the American; they shared the same human aspirations, dreamed the same dreams, laughed at the same jokes. Having viewed the ideological struggle from both sides, he suspected that the so-called "cold war" was largely manufactured and fueled by those few who stood to profit from it. However, he was trapped in a maze from which there seemed to be no exit except death . . . and, like most men, he did not consider that a viable option.

His first assignment was to pick up a packet of stolen documents and convey them, concealed in sample textbooks, by air to Mexico City. Although realizing that this action would commit him to the war as nothing heretofore, Eddie dared not refuse. He reported to Miami in bleak despair—and promptly contracted the worst cold of his life. (Perhaps the illness was largely psychosomatic, since depression often exhibits itself in physical terms.) The weather was as gloomy as his mood. His flight was delayed by a storm over the Gulf of Mexico. After waiting an hour on the runway for clearance, the aircraft returned to the terminal and the passengers debarked to wait still longer. Shivering with fever, Eddie lay down on a couch in the lounge and fell into a deep slumber. When he awoke, his flight had departed. He had slept through the summons of the public address system. He was now in worse trouble than before—the courier's merchandise had gone without the courier—but he was too sick to care. All he wanted was a bed. A taxi carried him to a nearby hotel, where he collapsed.

The following morning he felt sufficiently recovered to venture weakly downstairs with the intention of cabling his contact in Mexico City of the situation. A headline caught his eye: JET LINER VANISHES OVER GULF. It was his flight, the one he had missed, unreported and feared down at sea. Little hope was held for survivors due to the violent storm. His first thought was of his incredible good luck at having been spared . . . and then, reading further, he discovered that the list of presumed dead included the name of Edward T. Young.

The Coast Guard's search confirmed the first dire prediction. The airliner had gone down with all hands; some wreckage was found, but no bodies. Apparently the big jet had been torn apart by turbulence. The casualty list was made official and Edward T. Young, having once been listed on the passenger manifest and never removed, was part of it. Eighty-three names were added to the roll of those killed in aircraft accidents during 1965. Only one man knew that the figure was properly eighty-two.

The implications were staggering—and thrilling. The KGB, along with the rest of the world, would accept the fiction for fact. They would write off Eddie Young (and Pyotr Avanasov with him) with regret perhaps but no tears. His dream had come true. He was free!

At first he didn't know how to handle his freedom. Shortly he realized that it was not enough merely to die as Eddie Young. He must be born as someone else. His training at Middletown stood him in good stead. There he had been taught to create a fresh identity. He set out to create another. He began by destroying or discarding everything that might connect him with Eddie Young—documents, clothing, even toilet articles. He lightened his hair and darkened his skin; he added a mustache to his face and spectacles to his nose. He bought a bus ticket and left Miami. He had a destination in mind, although he did not yet know its precise location.

The bus deposited him in St. Louis. He lingered there only long enough to earn the price of a second ticket, which took him farther west. He roamed the American heartland for the next several months with apparent aimlessness, stopping frequently yet never very long. Money was a problem—he dared not tap Eddie Young's tidy bank account—but he was able to find employment, since willing workers are rare. His employers were usually reluctant to see him depart, and some made attractive offers to induce him to remain. "Guess I'll keep looking around," he told them to explain his refusal. They put him down as a likable drifter, seeking a nonexistent pot of gold at the end of the rainbow. None suspected that he was searching for something much more precious.

He found it at last in Prichard, Nebraska. The farming community was typical of the small towns which dotted the vast plains. The signboard on the outskirts proclaimed it "A Nice Place to Live," and once it had been just that. Now few believed so, particularly the young. Prichard was slowly dying, a victim of the mass exodus from the land to the city. Formerly the county seat, even this distinction had been wrested from it by an upstart neighbor following the burning of the courthouse several years earlier. A terrible tragedy that, what with the official records and vital statistics of a century going up in smoke. . . . Birth certificates too? Everything, mister—why, if a body didn't have his family Bible, he'd have the devil's own time proving he was even born!

Eddie courted the older residents assiduously and they, flattered by his interest, talked willingly of the past. From the chaff of their recollections he patiently gleaned the grain he sought. There had been a family named Towers —rather uppity folks, kept to themselves pretty much— who had moved away during the war; reckon they must be dead by now. Any children? Yep, there was a boy, a sickly youngster—matter of fact, he'd be about your age, that is, if he's still alive. What was his name now? No one was quite sure.

And so Paul Towers was born. Not in Prichard, of course, but in Denver, which was his next stop. There he purchased an old Bible at a used bookstore and painstakingly forged the necessary entries in crabbed handwriting and faded ink. He used the Bible to establish his new identity and received the official documents that substantiated it. The Towers had been Methodists; their "son" joined that church and was baptized into it. He might have stayed in Denver indefinitely, but its proximity to the North American Air Defense Command, a prime KGB target, made him uneasy. Discovery by his enemies was a far-fetched possibility—but no more far-fetched than the accident that had allowed him to escape them. Paul Towers moved on.

Again his wandering, though apparently random, had a purpose. Earlier, he had sought a birthplace; now he sought a home. He drifted west until the Pacific Ocean raised a natural barrier to further migration. California's rootless society suited him. Most of the state's inhabitants had their origins elsewhere, and one more emigrant was unremarkable. If the KGB operated there, it was not likely that the local apparatus had ever heard of Eddie Young.

Nevertheless, he avoided the larger cities where among their millions he might encounter a familiar, and hence unwelcome, face. Following the highway which skirted the sea, he arrived in Orchestra Beach late one Saturday evening. The lovely little coastal community, set apart from the mainstream but still moving with its own dynamic rhythm, reminded him oddly of Middletown. His odyssey was over; Paul Towers felt that he had come home.

The following day, a quiet Sunday, he set out on foot to explore this new haven, satisfaction growing steadily. His steps led him past the Presbyterian church where a placard advertised a Bach chorale, public invited. His fondness for Bach, that disciplined genius whose ordered harmonies struck a responsive chord in his own systematic nature, led him to accept the invitation. The choral interpretation of the master left much to be desired, but Paul was attracted to the soloist, a petite young redhead whose pert face was as charming as her soprano voice. The program identified her as Sybil Keller. After the performance, he lingered to pay his compliments.

"Sybil?" said the choir director. "Oh—I guess you want Sibby."

"Yes," Paul agreed slowly. "I guess I do."

What causes men to fall in love? The reasons are probably as numerous as the men themselves. The process whereby a male chooses one particular female in preference to all others (and vice versa) is inexplicable even to the two persons involved. Certainly, no one ever decides to fall in love; one merely discovers that he has. Certainly, also, everyone has countless opportunities to succumb and resists them. So it seems likely that timing is the key, that there comes a psychological moment when the human animal is vulnerable to the virus—and all the customary explanations ("She was beautiful" or "He was charming") are only ex post facto rationalizations.

For Paul Towers, the psychological moment arrived when he met Sybil Keller. She was pretty—but he had known prettier girls. Her nature was compatible with his —but no more so than others in the past, including Alice. And love was not part of his blueprint for the future (marriage, perhaps, but that was something else altogether). Nevertheless, he fell and, because it was for the first time, fell hard. There were a dozen valid arguments against his loving Sibby, or anyone, but they shattered before his desire.

Four months later, he married her. Time appeared to vindicate his impulsiveness. The old apprehension lingered for a time, but it gradually ebbed as a year passed and then another and another. Pyotr Avanasov was dead and so was Eddie Young; Paul Towers was alive and well and living in Orchestra Beach, California. A residue of caution remained—he could not yet bring himself to have children, that ultimate commitment to the future—but by July, 1970, he could believe that he had buried the past forever.

And then suddenly, from the pages of a dead man's appointment book, the past sprang back to horrifying life in the shape of two small houses—or barns. . . .

# EITHER/OR

"Brother!" Joe Chalk muttered when it appeared that Paul had finished his story. "I've never seen baloney sliced so thin or stacked so high in all my life."

"You mean you don't believe me?"

"I didn't say that. But now that you mention it, why should I? You haven't given me a single bit of proof."

"Will my dead body do? That's the only proof you're likely to get."

Chalk chewed on that. "I guess it all could have happened the way you claim. Let's stipulate for the time being that it did happen that way. What's this deal you mentioned a while back?"

"I supposed that was obvious. If you can help me save my life, I think I can help you catch the KGB agents you're after." Paul added, "Let me make myself clear. When I say 'save my life' I don't mean just keep me breathing. I mean save the life I've built here in Orchestra Beach."

"Sanctuary could be arranged, I guess. It's been done before."

"I want more than sanctuary. I want to be forgotten—by you as well as the KGB."

"What a man wants and what a man has to settle for aren't always the same thing," Chalk observed. "Anyhow, I like to see the merchandise before I talk price."

"Okay. In some way—God only knows how—the KGB discovered that Paul Towers just might be their late lamented comrade Eddie Young. They checked into me until they were convinced. That credit investigation was part of it and I'm sure there was more, because they're a thorough bunch. When they were absolutely sure, they gave orders to kill me. Why?"

"Punishment for defecting," Chalk suggested.

"They're too pragmatic to indulge in vengeance for vengeance's sake. It's simply not professional. Paul Towers wasn't doing them any harm. I'm not saying that they wouldn't gladly punish me if the opportunity arose. But to plan and attempt my execution, not once but three times, that wasn't to punish me. That was to protect them. They wanted me dead so badly that they even went to the trouble of importing their top disposal man—Nylec, the fellow who braced me tonight in town—to make sure the job was handled properly. So why am I such a threat to them? Vandamm's appointment book makes it obvious. Bob Barnes is in charge of the KGB effort to penetrate the SWORD project. And Bob is afraid that I might recognize him and ruin his game."

"Strikes me he'd figure just the opposite. If you did spot Barnes, you couldn't expose him without exposing yourself."

"Remember that I fooled them once by breaking from the norm. I might do it again. With so much riding on it, why take the chance? Safer to kill me and be sure. But by a fluke, Nylec blew it."

"Okay, what's their next move?"

"They don't have a choice. They'll have to keep trying. And since I can't run and I can't hide, I don't have a choice either. I've got to get them before they get me. The only weapon I have is that I can identify Bob Barnes."

"What makes you think you'll get the chance? There's nothing to indicate that Barnes is in Orchestra Beach. He may be calling the shots from L.A. It's only a few miles away. There are over four million people in L.A. I can't line them all up for you."

"Bob is here. This whole thing doesn't make sense otherwise."

"It doesn't make sense anywise. But let's say that Barnes is here. You figure on standing on the corner in hopes he may drive by?" Chalk snorted. "Get lost, Towers—or whatever your name is. You don't have anything to sell."

Paul said, studying him, "You don't like me, do you?"

"I got no use for defectors—from either side. You all stink."

"No, it's not just that I defected. I think what really bugs you is that I did so well at it. Pretty wife, good job, comfortable life . . . It doesn't seem fair, does it? I should be cowering in a swamp someplace like a terrified rat."

Chalk regarded him in grim silence. He said reluctantly, "Maybe I would like to see you get racked up. But I never let personal feelings interfere with my job."

Paul shrugged. "There's no reason we have to be friends, just allies. Mutual benefit is the only real basis for a partnership, anyway."

"Not so fast—partner. You haven't explained yet how you intend to find Barnes, particularly now when he knows you're wise to him."

"Well, I can't just wander around looking for him, you're right about that. I'll have to make him come to me."

"You mean use yourself as bait? Barnes will send somebody else, probably that Nylec fellow, to spring the trap. I know I would."

"Not if you believed that I was more use to you alive than dead. Put yourself in Bob's shoes. What's the one thing you want more than anything else at the moment? To get the plans for the new sonar, right? Now if you believed that Paul Towers could steal them for you—"

"You'd have a hell of a time selling him that."

"Suppose I could tell him that I'm Victor Vandamm's replacement at Keller Corp?" He grinned at Chalk's startled expression. "After all, Hank did make me a legitimate offer—and the offer's still open."

"Nothing doing," Chalk declared flatly. "Put a Soviet agent in such a sensitive position? I'd have to be out of my bloody head."

"A former Soviet agent," Paul corrected.

"That's your story. I don't trust you farther than I can throw this motel. You could still be working for the other side."

Paul sighed. "I'm not working for either side. I'm in business for myself. I don't want any part of your international chess game. I want to live like a human being, not a pawn, in a world where nobody bothers to steal secrets because there aren't any secrets worth stealing. Where there'd be no use for agents like Bob Barnes—or Joe Chalk."

"That kind of world never has existed and never will. We haven't come so far from the cave in the past million years. We still grab anything we're strong enough to hold and we still stomp on anyone who tries to take it away from us. Hell, isn't that exactly what you're doing now? You were plenty willing to sit out this war as long as it cost you nothing. But let someone shake your cozy little tree and then it's quick, where do I go to enlist?"

"Any man will fight for his own life. Can't you see the difference?"

"What I see is that you're a man who wants it both ways. Lots of luck. You'll need it."

"That mean you're turning down my proposition?"

"I'm putting you under arrest, Towers. Illegal entry, failure to register as the agent of a foreign power, maybe more. You'll be safe in prison. The KGB won't be able to get at you there. And you won't be able to hurt the U.S., either."

"You're not arresting me," Paul said calmly. "You don't have a case. I'll deny everything and you'll have one hell of a time proving it. Even if you can, what good is that going to do you? I may be in prison . . . but Bob Barnes won't be."

There was a long silence. Chalk broke it with a grudging compliment. "You're a cool customer, I got to say that for you. Shrewd, too. You figure I want Barnes so bad I can taste him, don't you? But if I go along with you, I'm putting my own head on the block."

Paul waited while the other man grappled with his dilemma. He was confident of the outcome. Chalk, like all his breed whatever their nationality, was a gambler with the gambler's passion for the game. To throw in a promising hand, no matter what the odds, was unthinkable. Chalk signified his intention to play with a threat. "If you cross me—if you even zig when you should have zagged—you won't have to worry about the KGB. I'll cash you in myself. Clear?"

"I'd have to be pretty stupid to double-cross the only

friend I've got, wouldn't I?" Paul smiled thinly. "Even if said friend hates my guts."

"Okay, then. What's our first move? How do you intend to get in touch with Barnes?"

"Through the newspapers. That's my move. Your move is not to move at all. Oh, you'd better arrange to get the police off my back. That shouldn't be hard for a man with your connections. After that, sit tight. Don't try to contact me—and don't pull any cute stunts like putting me under surveillance. Barnes has more savvy than both of us put together, plus the kind of intuition women only think they have. He's bound to be suspicious. If he gets the slightest notion that I'm conning him, I'm as good as dead."

Chalk pursed his lips dubiously. "If Barnes is as brainy as you claim, you're as good as dead already."

"I fooled him once before. I'm egotistic enough to believe that I can do it again." Paul glanced at his watch. "Four o'clock already. Funny how time flies when you're enjoying yourself. I've got to get home before Sibby wakes up and misses me. She mustn't know anything about this —for her safety as well as mine."

Chalk halted him at the doorway. "One thing that bothers me. How did you find out I was Division Five? Not even your brother-in-law knows that."

"Doesn't Division Five keep mug files on the opposition? So does the KGB. People in our profession can't afford to forget a face. But I never actually met you until the other night."

"I thought that maybe I'd forgotten yours. I was afraid I might be losing my grip."

"I hope to God you haven't," Paul told him. "For both our sakes."

Sibby reached out a hand as she frequently did upon awaking—and invariably following intercourse—to touch her husband's flesh and recapture the intimacy that sleep had interrupted. Her fingers encountered only the sheet and it was cold. "Honey?" she murmured and then, suddenly remembering her dream, sat bolt upright. "Paul! Where are you?"

The bed was empty and so was the bath. The clock told her it was nearly eight. Paul seldom left for work before nine (and never without kissing her good-by) but she could detect no reassuring sounds from the other part of the house to indicate his presence. Sibby scrambled out of bed, alarmed less by the dream than by her recollection of the events which had preceded it, Paul's odd behavior, the visit from the police . . . She was nearly running by the time she reached the kitchen.

"The house on fire?" Paul greeted her abrupt appearance.

"Paul! Where'd you go?"

"What kind of a question is that? I've been right here, having a cup of coffee. What's bothering you, Sibby?"

She put her arms around him, drawing reassurance from the familiar solidity of his body. "I had the strangest dream and when I woke up and you weren't there . . . You're all right, aren't you, darling?"

"I'm fine." He looked it. His gaze was steady, his voice calm; no trace remained of the inexplicable anxiety that had racked him on the previous evening.

"Aren't you tired, though? You were so beat last night, more than I've ever seen you. You should have stayed in bed a while longer. Particularly since you can go in late today."

"As a matter of fact, I may not go in today at all."

"Really?" Sibby said, worry returning. It was not like her husband to stay away from the office on a working day. She probed with a joke. "Aren't you afraid the boss will fire you? I hear he's a slave driver."

"A real Simon Legree. That's why I've decided to quit." He saw that she didn't understand. "I'm taking the job with Keller Corp. I just got through talking on the phone with Hank."

"Paul, do you mean it? Oh, honey, that's wonderful! What did Hank say? I'll bet he was tickled pink."

"Well, you know your brother. All he said was 'Good, how soon can you start?'"

"I still can't believe it. When did you decide?" Before he could answer, her excitement diminished and she asked anxiously, "I didn't push you into doing something you really don't want, did I? I'd never expect you to sacrifice your principles because I—"

"Principles are fine when you can afford them. I weighed mine and decided they were a luxury. You were right. There's no future in my present situation. With this new job there may be."

"You don't sound too convinced."

"Well, when you deal with the government—any government—it's here today and gone tomorrow. I may not last long enough with Keller Corp to get my name on the door."

"No, sir!" Sibby declared positively. "You'll show them. You can lick the world." She began to waltz him around the kitchen, chanting, "We're going to be rich! We're going to be rich!"

"Not so fast," he admonished, laughing. "I haven't even discussed salary with Hank yet."

"Oh, I'm sure it'll be something fabulous! Paul, let's go out and celebrate!"

"Sorry, hon. I've got to start disposing of the *Dispatch*. Did you forget we still own a newspaper? By an odd coincidence, I heard just this week that somebody may be interested in buying us out. So I've got some phone calls to make."

"Me, too. I want to tell everybody I know about your new job." Sibby hesitated. "It's all right if I brag a little, isn't it? Of course, if it's supposed to be a secret—"

"Go ahead and brag all you want. It'll be in the afternoon paper, anyway. But before you start the grapevine buzzing, what say you slip on some clothes and fix my breakfast?"

"Ring for the cook," Sibby replied grandly. "Oh, dear me, I forgot. It's her day out. I suppose I'll have to do it myself. Noblesse oblige and all that."

She gathered her robe about her and swept regally out of the kitchen. But once in the bedroom she leaped onto the bed and bounced upon it with the exuberance of a child on Christmas morning. Outside the window the sun was shining, but even without its cheerful radiance life had never looked quite so bright to her.

The bank did not open its doors for business until ten o'clock, but most of the employees were at work by nine and some earlier. "Good morning?" George Dickman replied to Paul's greeting. "Who the hell says so?"

"My, my. Sounds like you're a bit hung over today, buddy."

"A bit? Yeah, the same way that the North Pole is a bit chilly. I wish I were there right now. I wish I were anywhere except here. The only thing that keeps me going is the possibility that I may get to foreclose a mortgage or repossess a few cars."

"Since you're in such a good mood, I'm going to let you

do me a favor. Remember that credit investigator? I need to know his name, after all."

"I wish you'd make up your damn mind," George grumbled. "First you do, then you don't, then you do . . . You're worse than a dame and nowhere near as much fun. Sorry, pal, I threw the guy's card away."

"Look in your wastebasket." There was a silence. "Well?"

"All right, I looked. It's empty. The janitor dumped it yesterday."

"When's your trash pickup?"

"How the hell would I know? That's the one thing—maybe the only thing—that the assistant manager isn't responsible for."

"If you're on the same schedule as the *Dispatch,* your trash day isn't until tomorrow. So trot out to the alley and find that card for me."

"Have you blown your mind? Do your own scavenging."

"George, I'm asking as your friend."

"What does it cost to buy back my introduction? Okay, friend, hold on for a minute." It was closer to ten before he returned to the telephone and his voice was more disgruntled than before. "Well, I hope you're satisfied. There I was in the alley, up to my navel in garbage, when the big brass from the main office drove in. Can you imagine what they thought? I can see it on my record now. Under special interests: Ragpicking!"

"That'd look better than your real special interests. Did you find the card?"

"Yeah, I found it. On the very bottom, naturally." Paul wrote down the name: Daniel Redstone, Southland Investigation Service. The address was on Flower Street in downtown Los Angeles. "Now do you mind telling me what's so damn important about it?"

140

"Turns out it wasn't important at all," Paul lied blandly. "I just thought it might be. Sorry to have bothered you." He hung up on George's infuriated bellow. He fancied he could hear it anyway, even without the aid of the telephone.

He lied to Sibby also. "Looks promising for a sale. I've got to take a run into L.A. this morning and see what kind of a deal they'll offer me. Don't get your hopes up, though. It may amount to nothing."

She rejected his warning; this was a day for dreaming. "Oh, I know you'll get everything you want. It was just meant to be, that's all!"

Paul could not share her optimism. Watching the freeway unwind before him, he was tempted to pursue it to its distant end, wherever that might be. But running away had not saved him before, even under vastly more favorable conditions. Now that both camps were aware of his existence, flight was only a temporary panacea, not a cure. Furthermore, there was Sibby. He could give up all else. He could not give up his wife, not while the slimmest chance remained that he might keep her. He was bound by love, the strongest shackle of all.

He made certain that the enemy was not on his tail. He couldn't be equally certain that he wouldn't find the enemy waiting for him when he arrived. The Southland Investigation Service was an apparently legitimate firm, listed in the yellow pages and commended by the Better Business Bureau. Possibly the KGB had hired it to do their legwork. On the other hand, it might well be a KGB front operation. But since it was his only lead to Bob Barnes, he had no choice but to risk it.

The weathered stone building wore the architectural gingerbread popular at the turn of the century. Once the belle of the ball, now a faded spinster, she had lost her stylishness but not her dignity. Southland Investigation Service occupied a fourth-floor suite which consisted of a high-ceilinged anteroom ruled by a plump secretary-receptionist and a smaller private office for her boss, the owner of the agency and its sole operative as well.

Daniel Redstone was a heavy-set man of sixty, as gray as the stone walls and nearly as durable. His speech and bearing proved that he had been a police officer as much as the departmental certificate of service and a clutch of commendations framed on the walls. His keen eyes had viewed the entire catalogue of human frailty; his large mouth could still smile about it. Redstone was obviously not overburdened with work, yet his manner suggested that he would not appreciate having his time wasted. Paul came straight to the point. "My name is Paul Towers," he said as soon as he seated himself in the not-too-comfortable visitor's chair. "I live in Orchestra Beach. You ran a credit investigation on me a week or so ago."

Redstone matched his bluntness. "That's correct. What can I do for you, Mr. Towers?"

"I need to know who hired you to make the investigation of me."

"Can't tell you that." He pointed at the agency plaque which proclaimed Investigations Handled Discreetly & Confidentially. To demonstrate that his refusal carried no hostility, Redstone added, "I can tell you that my report contained nothing damaging, if that's what you're concerned about."

Paul decided to put his cards on the table. "I'm not worried about my reputation. I am worried about my life. Someone is trying to kill me and I'm sure that your client is involved." He saw the skepticism in the other man's face. "No, I can't prove it. But listen to me for a minute. Did you read about the murder of a man named Fred Rossi the other night?"

In his pocket was the newspaper clipping, should it be necessary. It remained there. "I keep up on these things," Redstone said. "Old times' sake, I guess. Don't recall your name being mentioned, though."

"It wasn't. Neither was the fact that Rossi looked a lot like me—or that he was driving my car at the time he was shot. On top of that, there have been two other attempts on my life, one before Rossi, one since."

"How come you haven't told the police about it? I figure you haven't because you're here instead of them."

"They wouldn't believe me. The police suspect that I'm the one who killed Rossi."

"Are you?" Redstone accepted his denial with a smile that expressed derision for the question rather than the answer. "Could hardly expect you to say yes, could I? But why should I believe you when the police won't?"

"I can't think of a single reason," Paul admitted candidly. "I just hope you will."

Redstone chuckled. "Well, you're honest about it. Don't see much of that anymore. Everybody's throwing curves. Of course, honesty may be *your* curve. Tell me more. You claim somebody's out to get you. Who?"

"I don't have a name, not yet. That's what I want from you." Paul took out his wallet. "I'll pay for any help you can give me, naturally."

"Put your money away. I don't have anything against being paid for my help, but I can't sell what you want to buy. Working for both sides is considered unethical." He cocked an eyebrow at Paul's smile. "That strike you funny?"

"A private joke. All right, Mr. Redstone, I'll ask it as a favor—one human being to another."

Redstone regarded him thoughtfully, blunt fingers drumming on the desktop. He went to the filing cabinet in a corner of the office, unlocked it and withdrew a manila folder. He read the contents standing while Paul watched him anxiously. At last, Redstone said, "I don't see any tie-in here at all."

"Would you allow me to be the judge of that? I hate to sound melodramatic, but my life may depend on it."

Redstone grimaced, plainly in a quandary. "You sell real good. And I sure don't have eyes to get mixed up in a homicide case. That's no business for a private detective, never mind what they try to hand you on TV. By the same token, I don't have any right to violate the confidence of a client, either."

"I promise that I'll never tell anyone where I got the information."

"Maybe not. But res ipsa loquitur, as they say in court. The thing speaks for itself. If it gets around that Dan Redstone can't keep his lip buttoned, I'm finished." He closed the folder decisively. "Sorry. As a human being I'd like to help you. As a businessman I can't."

Paul eyed the folder, wondering if he might be able to snatch it from the strong hands. Before he could reach a decision, Redstone said, "I might be able to give you some professional advice that didn't involve breaking a trust. Stick around while I go to the john and we'll talk about it. This damn prostate . . ." He tossed the folder onto the desk in front of Paul and strode out of the office.

"Thanks," Paul murmured. The purpose of Redstone's trip to the bathroom was clear and had nothing to do with his prostate. Redstone could not ethically give him the information. But if Paul chose to sneak a look at the file in his absence . . . He snatched up the folder. He did not bother to read the entire report, since only the addressee was significant: Muse, Oatis & Associates, Beverly Hills.

He left fifty dollars on the desktop but no note of gratitude, although he was grateful enough. A note would implicate Redstone, at least in his own conscience. Money, on the other hand, was mute; it could even have blown in through the open window.

The announcement of his new position was buried on the financial page of the afternoon newspaper. Paul was not in the least disturbed by the story's lack of prominence. He had phoned it in himself early that morning past the normal deadline and only by cashing in past favors had he persuaded the city editor to accept it. So he did not grumble at the size of the item; he was grateful that it was there at all.

Daniel Redstone, wittingly or otherwise, had given him a lead. He set about to follow it. His first move was to explore the resources of the public library, where an hour's delving into the city directory and other sources informed him that Muse, Oatis & Associates were brokers in the import-export business, specializing in trade with Australia, Japan and Southeast Asia. The firm was young, less than two years in operation, yet Dun & Bradstreet rated them highly and a stockbroker he called likewise had nothing detrimental to report.

Paul's second move was to reconnoiter his presumed enemy's headquarters but at a cautious distance. Muse, Oatis maintained a suite of offices high in a Wilshire Boulevard bank building several light years removed in prestige and affluence from the shabby structure he had visited earlier. The brokerage business was apparently legitimate, at least on the surface; a phone call pretending to inquire about the purchase and shipment of New Zealand wool was handled knowledgeably. Yet Muse, Oatis was exactly the type of front that the KGB favored, since it provided a convenient channel for the flow of information, materiel and personnel in and out of the country. Nordstrom and Whited, his former employers, had been such a cover operation; Paul felt convinced that Muse, Oatis was another. Certainly, he could imagine no innocent reason why a company engaged in overseas trade would take an interest in a small-town newspaper publisher to the extent of hiring a private detective to investigate him. He wondered if Redstone had noted the anomaly also and if this had prompted his covert assistance.

Whether Muse, Oatis was what it professed to be or something more sinister was a question he dared not pursue directly. Bob Barnes might be Muse or Oatis or one of the anonymous Associates . . . but the success of Paul's gamble hinged on making Barnes come to him, not vice versa.

His final move was to bait the hook. At a messenger service he prepared an envelope addressed to his one-time mentor and present adversary, care of the brokerage firm. In the envelope he placed the clipping from the financial page and his business card with his home telephone number circled. On the card he wrote four words: *Better Red than dead.*

The sclerotic freeways were clogged, bumper-to-bumper, until they resembled slow-moving conveyer belts rather than the high-speed avenues they were intended to be. It took Paul over two hours to reach home, and since the messenger service had promised to deliver the letter to Muse, Oatis in a fraction of that time, his first question to Sibby was "Any calls?"

"Simply dozens," she told him, weary but cheerful. "I spent all morning telling all our friends the good news. At least, I thought I'd told them all. The past couple of hours the phone has practically been ringing off the hook from the ones I missed."

"Nobody else—just friends?"

"Sure, there was a real estate agent who'd heard we might be selling the house—I still haven't figured out where he got that idea—and a man who wanted to talk to you about mutual funds. And I just this minute got off the phone with a reporter from the *Wall Street Journal*. He'd read about you in the L.A. paper and wanted more facts. I gave him enough information about you to fill a book. That was all right, wasn't it? You said I could brag as much as I wanted."

"So I did. Don't be disappointed if the *Journal* doesn't use a word of it, though." Paul doubted if the reporter actually worked for the financial daily, or any publication. The timing of the call argued that it was the enemy, seeking collaborative information.

Sibby was eager for a progress report. Had he sold the *Dispatch*? No, but he hadn't really expected to, not immediately; these things took time. He assured her that, all in all, his day had been profitable. He had put out the proper feelers, let the interested parties know that he was willing to deal. The next move was up to them. "I'll have to babysit the phone day and night in case they call."

"They surely wouldn't phone you at night, would they?"

"The people I'm dickering with don't observe normal business hours."

Sibby was mildly chagrined. "I was hoping we might celebrate by going out to dinner. I didn't defrost a thing. Oh, well, if you don't mind TV dinners and beer instead of steaks and champagne. . . . Maybe it's just as well. I've got that darn choir practice at eight o'clock."

As she pointed out afterward, they could have dined at a restaurant, anyway, since the telephone remained silent. They ate the TV dinners (which these days were seldom consumed in front of the television set) and Paul promised her a bigger celebration later "when we've really got something to celebrate."

"Don't you think we have enough already?"

"I guess I feel there's still too much hanging over our heads."

Sibby assumed that he was referring to the sale of the *Dispatch*. "I don't want you fretting about it," she told him as she departed for the church. "And quit hovering over that phone. It'll ring when it's darn good and ready and not before. Read a book while I'm gone or watch TV, anything to take your mind off business, promise?"

Paul gave her his word—and broke it before she was out the door. The "business" she commanded him to forget was his life (and, to some extent, hers as well). Nothing less than a frontal lobotomy could erase it from his thoughts. The next few hours were crucial. He felt sure that Bob Barnes would act swiftly to accept the bait or to reject it. Barnes was not the sort who dithered over decisions. If his answer was affirmative, the telephone would ring, and shortly. If negative, the assassin would deliver it with equal dispatch. Since the odds were no better than even either way, Paul prepared for each contingency. He closed the windows and locked the doors, turned on the outdoor lights and extinguished those inside. There were no guns in the house; he armed himself with a boning knife. It would be scant use against a pistol, but the sharp blade gave him some comfort, however false. His senses were a far better weapon. With the discipline learned so long ago, he tuned himself to the sounds of the night, establishing a mental trip wire which an intruder would set twanging.

He could not read his wrist watch in the gloom, but he was aware of the passing of each minute. Eight-thirty came and, went, nine, nine-thirty . . . His confidence, shaky at best, began to ebb away. His proposal had been in the enemy's hands for six hours. Continued silence argued that they had spurned it. He wondered whatever had prompted him to expect otherwise. What conceit to believe that he the novice might trick Barnes the master, Barnes who possessed the keenest intelligence he had ever encountered, and instincts that were keener still! Of course, Barnes had seen through the pitiful masquerade. Paul could almost hear the lazily scornful voice: "Sorry about that, Eddie. Nice try, though."

"Damn you," Paul whispered in reply. "I'm not dead yet." He didn't have to wait meekly for Nylec to deliver the coup de grâce. He'd phone Joe Chalk instead, admit failure and request protective custody. The consequences —well, he didn't care to think about them, but at least they did not include immediate death. Sibby would be home from choir practice shortly after ten. If he hadn't heard from Barnes by then . . .

He sat beside the silent instrument like a man keeping vigil over a loved one he is powerless to save yet whose passing he feels compelled to witness. At last he heard the Toyota turn into the driveway. That does it, he thought— as a doctor might pronounce life extinct—and placed his hand on the telephone.

It rang. Paul jerked his hand back instinctively, as if the instrument had snapped at him. Then a warm tide of elation rushed through him and though simultaneously bracing himself for disappointment—it could be anyone, even a wrong number—he seized the receiver. "Hello?"

The voice in his ear did not belong to Bob Barnes, but neither was it crushingly familiar. "Mr. Paul Towers?"

"This is Paul Towers."

"I wish to inform you that your letter was received and studied and that we find your proposition interesting."

"You're accepting it, then?"

"If you'd care to discuss it further, please be at the Los Angeles County Museum of Art at ten o'clock tomorrow morning."

Paul strove to keep his voice level. "Museum of Art, ten o'clock. Who do I meet there?"

His caller did not answer the question directly; he seemed to be reading from prepared instructions. "You will rent a tape recorder from the docent at the Ahmanson Gallery and follow the tour it suggests." He hung up without saying good-by.

Paul sat listening to the buzz of the dial tone. "Made it!" he breathed. Reaction struck him and his fingers commenced to tremble so violently he had difficulty replacing the receiver in its cradle. He managed to control both his muscles and his jubilation. He had taken the first trick and it was sweet to savor, but the hand was far from being played out. Yet he had nearly given up hope of taking any trick at all.

Sibby came in from the garage, turning on lights en route. She uttered a soft gasp of surprise to find him seated in the kitchen. "I supposed you'd gone to bed. What on earth are you doing here in the dark?"

"I was heading for the bedroom when the phone rang."

"Oh," she said, accepting the lie. Then remembering, "Oh! You mean those people finally did call? What'd they say? Was it good or bad?"

"Still too early to be sure. At least, they're nibbling.

They want to talk to me tomorrow. That means another trip to L.A."

"Oh, dear. Must you? All that freeway traffic . . . I know you're a good driver, darling, but I worry about the other guy. I swear that some of them behave as if they want to kill you."

"No doubt about it," Paul agreed. "But I don't intend to let them."

He arrived for his appointment at precisely ten o'clock the following morning—punctuality was a virtue stressed by all espionage services, since tardiness often equaled disaster—and with full cognizance of his danger. The rendezvous could well prove a trap; while conceiving himself the fisherman, he might turn out to be the fish instead.

The Museum of Art occupies a corner of Hancock Park adjacent to the famed La Brea Tar Pits. Rembrandt and Picasso and Henry Moore are now honored where woolly mammoths and saber-toothed tigers once roamed, demonstrating how far creation has evolved (although some critics of modern art suggest the opposite). The museum complex consists of three multi-level buildings whose gray concrete architecture can best be described as Library Modern, with a touch of Airport Terminal thrown in. Of the three, the Ahmanson Gallery is the largest and most frequented, since it contains the principal exhibition of art and artifacts.

Paul strode past the huge reflecting pool, whose twin fountains all too often caused the water to froth with detergent suds, and across the broad plaza. His business suit made him conspicuous among the casually garbed crowd which wandered amid the outdoor display of sculpture and statuary with expressions ranging from awe to derision. He wished his arrival to be observed and felt sure that it was, though by whom he could not tell. The old man sunning himself on the bench perhaps, or the student with his sketch pad . . . even someone at a window in the office building across the boulevard, through the telescopic sights of a rifle. He was relieved when the doors of the Ahmanson Gallery, closing behind him, ruled out that possibility.

The four-level gallery, built around a large central shaft onto which each level opened, hummed with the voices of adults, lowered in respect, and echoed with the footsteps of children, who felt no such compunction. Paul presented himself at the desk which faced the entrance and asked to rent a tape player.

The docent was a sleek matron whose muted knit suit matched the brown tones of the carpet. "Any particular level? Or would you prefer the grand tour?"

His orders had not been specific on that point. "I'll take the works." He signed the required form and watched her face as she read the name. Her expression didn't change.

The docent assisted him to don the purse-size player and to place the button in his ear, meanwhile explaining how the machine was operated. Unlike some galleries, the Ahmanson did not have radio transmitters embedded in the floor. The taped tour was designed to lead him from one room to the next at regular intervals; should he wish to linger past the normal time, he must be sure to press the Off button. "Otherwise, you'll wind up looking at the statue of the Goddess Hygeia while you're hearing a description of Van Dyck's self-portrait." The docent seemed disappointed when he failed to laugh.

Paul turned on the player with some anticipation, not knowing what he would hear, perhaps even Bob Barnes himself. What he did hear was exactly what he had paid to hear, nothing more. "Welcome to the Ahmanson Gallery of the Los Angeles County Museum of Art," the recorded voice, so carefully neuter that it might have been either masculine or feminine, greeted him. "For the next hour and one half it is your privilege to view one of the finest collections of art and art objects, ranging from the earliest primitive to the most sophisticated modern, to be found anywhere in the world. To begin your tour, the room you are entering houses the Samuel H. Kress collection devoted to the period of the Early Italian Renaissance . . ."

Since he had no notion of his ultimate destination, Paul allowed his disembodied guide to lead him by the hand. Or, more accurately, the ear; the two of them moved slowly through the maze of velvet-covered walls, progressing from Italian to Flemish and Dutch, then to the French masters of the eighteenth and nineteenth centuries and their English contemporaries, and finally to the elevator. Paul examined each painting while covertly scrutinizing the other spectators, some of whom wore tape players identical to his own. No one appeared to take a similar interest in him.

The third level was devoted to the work of more modern artists. Paul began this portion of the tour with rekindled anticipation. Not only did he favor the French impressionist above all others but, more importantly, so did Bob Barnes. This particular corner of the gallery seemed a fitting meeting place. Fitting or not, Barnes was not there.

The fourth level proved no more productive. His watch informed him that an hour had passed. He commenced to suspect that he had wasted it. Failure to make contact by now argued that no contact had been planned and that the exercise was designed to test his good faith. The bland voice in his ear, which Paul was learning to detest, directed him to the bottom level.

A blonde woman in sunglasses and a print frock came

trotting from the direction of the Fashion Group Gallery to join him in the elevator. "I'm going all the way down," Paul informed her, finger poised above the floor selector panel. "How about you?"

The young woman removed the dark glasses. "Hello, Eddie," she said quietly.

The muscles of his throat contracted, reducing his reply to a whisper. "Hello, Alice."

They drank coffee on the terrace of the museum cafeteria. Anyone observing them might have concluded that here were two old friends, met by chance after a long separation. Like most who recall an intimacy blighted by time, they found communication difficult. Their conversation stumbled rather than galloped ("Well, how have you been?" "Fine, thanks—and you?"), punctuated by silences during which they glanced uneasily at the other patrons or the statues of the prehistoric monsters which dotted the park grounds or at their cups—anywhere but at each other, as if they might read in the other's eyes something better forgotten.

Yet it could not be ignored, however painful. Paul finally forced them to confront it. "Not much like the old days in Middletown, is it?" he said with a wan smile. "Do you ever think of them, Alice?"

"Now and then. You've changed a great deal, Eddie."

"You haven't," he lied. "You're still as pretty as ever." Why reveal the truth, that he scarcely recognized her? It was more than the change of hair color, more than the California tan, more even than the ravages of time. Her transformation had been internal. Paul remembered her as a vibrant girl, younger than he. Now she was unquestionably older, a woman weary and with-drawn. Only six years . . . they had obviously been difficult years for Alice.

"I hear you're married," she said, toying with her spoon.

"That's right. And you?"

"In a way." Since she wore a wedding band, Paul interpreted her answer to mean that she was masquerading as another agent's wife, as she had once masqueraded as his. "Any children?"

"Not yet." No need to ask her the same question; her work precluded motherhood. He sensed that she desired it otherwise and he was angered by a world which forbade her even to hope for fulfillment as a woman. "I've always wanted to be able to tell you that I got your note. It touched me deeply."

"I wondered if you did." Then she shrugged. "It was a foolish thing to do. I was very young in those days. I believed that love was important. I know better now. All that's really important is staying alive."

"That's what I'm trying to do. I suppose you know that our mutual friends have tried to kill me."

He was oddly relieved to read shock in her expression. "No, I didn't know. I wasn't even aware that you were still alive until last night—I heard about the plane crash years ago, of course—and when I was ordered to meet you—"

"Why you, of all people? Why didn't Bob come?"

"I suppose he believes that you'd be less likely to betray me than him in case you meant to set a trap. Or perhaps it was his macabre sense of humor. God knows I didn't want the assignment. But orders are orders."

"What other orders did Bob give you?"

"To ask you certain questions." She paused as if to arrange them in the proper sequence. "First, how did you find out about Muse, Oatis? Did the investigator Redstone tell you?"

"Redstone refused to tell me a thing." It wasn't precisely a lie and he wished to protect the man who had befriended him. "He happens to have weak kidneys. While he was in the bathroom, I peeked in his files."

"Who knows about your past association with Bob?"

"No one."

"Not even your wife?"

"Especially not my wife. She—and everybody else—believes that I'm Paul Towers from Prichard, Nebraska, and I've never been within ten thousand miles of the Soviet Union."

"All right," Alice said, moving on to the next question. "Why do you want to come back to"—she hesitated—"to us?"

"Hell, I don't want to come back—and Bob must know it. It's the only way I can see to save my skin. He tell you what he's after, the new sonar? Well, I've got the map to the treasure. Not only am I the project manager for SWORD but I'm also the big boss's favorite in-law. If I can't get the plans, nobody can. Is Bob interested in my proposition?"

"I'm authorized to tell you that he is very interested. Providing your terms are acceptable."

"My terms are simple enough. I supply the plans to him. He forgets about me."

"Is that all?" Her tone told him that she considered him incredibly naive. The KGB might permit him to live, but once having found a valuable tool they would continue to employ it as long as any value remained. Paul understood that as well as she, but to pretend otherwise rendered his behavior more credible.

He said, "The only thing I've ever wanted was to be left alone."

"Poor Eddie," she murmured. "I knew, even back in Middletown, that you didn't have any heart for this cruel business. Haven't you learned yet that the one thing the world will never do is leave you alone?"

He was grateful for the thinly veiled warning, but he feigned obtuseness. "I don't see why not. If Bob accepts my terms—"

"Oh, he will," Alice said with a sigh for his folly. "I wouldn't be here otherwise. But remember what I said, Eddie." Her voice became businesslike; once again she seemed to be referring to memorized instructions. "You will go home and resume a normal life. Don't attempt to contact Muse, Oatis. When you're ready to deliver the merchandise, place a classified ad in both daily papers. 'I am responsible for no debts except my own.' Sign it Edward T. Young."

Paul was forced to smile at this latest example of Barnes' humor. "Very appropriate. But tell Bob that I insist on dealing with him personally when the time comes. I won't turn over the plans—and my life—to a man I don't know."

"I'll tell him—but I think I'll use 'prefer' rather than 'insist.' You've been away from this business for quite a while, but you should remember that those in your position don't insist on anything." She pushed back her chair. "I must go."

Paul rose also. They stood gazing at each other for a moment in a silence born of a wistful sorrow at what they had once been to each other, were no longer and could never be again. Alice finally broke it. "Tell me," she said softly. "Is she—nice?"

There was no need to ask whom she meant. "Yes," Paul said. "She's very nice. In fact, she reminds me of a girl I knew a long time ago, a girl named Irina."

He told the girl named Sibby that the hoped-for sale of the newspaper had fallen through, after all. She was properly disappointed and concerned. "What are we going to do, Paul? Gosh, if we can't get rid of the *Dispatch*—"

"Don't worry, hon. I'll think of something."

He already had; the following morning he took Tom Easley out for coffee and proposed what he had intended from the beginning. Easley was so startled that for once he forgot to be flippant. "Me buy the *Dispatch*? You've got to be kidding!"

"You've always wanted your own paper. Here's your opportunity."

"Aren't you forgetting something—like money? I don't know what price you're putting on the *Dispatch*, but I'm sure it's over five thousand bucks and that's all I've got to my name."

Paul agreed to accept the five thousand as a down payment and Easley's note for the balance, to be redeemed in installments out of income. It was an exceedingly generous arrangement, but Easley's gratitude helped alleviate his regret at relinquishing the *Dispatch*. It seemed almost as if he were selling a member of the family. Yet sell it he must, and since it was an ill wind that blew no one good . . .

Sibby put it in happier perspective. "How perfect!" she exclaimed when he told her. "Sure, maybe we could get more money by holding onto it for a while longer— but how often do you get the chance to make a man's dreams come true? And you're leaving the *Dispatch* in good hands. I'd say it was a happy ending all the way around."

Not quite all the way; for Wynne, the change of ownership was the last in a series of shattering blows. Easley offered to keep her on but she declined politely, went home and attempted to kill herself with sleeping capsules. Prompt treatment saved her life. The doctors were less sure of her sanity. They spoke of emotional exhaustion and depressive psychosis and urged extended therapy. An innocent victim of a war she hadn't even known was going on . . . Sibby, who visited her, remarked to Paul that Wynne had aged ten years.

Another victim of that same war—though not quite so innocent—remained in a different sort of limbo. The corpse of Fred Rossi, released by the coroner, lay in the county morgue waiting for someone to claim it. Rossi had no living relatives save his widow (it was doubtful whether Wynne bore any legal responsibility even if her condition had permitted her to shoulder it) and no friends, either. Burial at public expense seemed the body's likely fate, once the proscribed waiting period was over. In death as in life, others would pay Fred Rossi's bills.

His murder had long since ceased to be newsworthy. The sheriff's terse statement—the investigation was continuing routinely—was accepted by the newspapers for what it was, an admission of failure. Just another unsolved homicide; ho-hum. Orchestra Beach was too busy playing host to thousands of live strangers to worry about a single dead one.

Even Sibby, who grieved over each fallen sparrow, could summon up no sympathy for Rossi. "Look what he did to poor Wynne." ("Poor Wynne" was now nearly one word in her vocabulary, like damyankee.) "Some people actually seem destined for tragedy, though. Poor Wynne . . . all she did was to fall in love—twice—and both times with the wrong man. It's sad."

"Sure, but I don't see what I can do about it."

"Don't get the idea that I'm blaming you, darling. You can't help it if you're irresistible." Sibby eyed him impishly. "But if you don't mind, I think I'll choose your next secretary myself."

She didn't, however, and neither did Paul. Nora Queen was already on the job when he reported to Keller Corp the following Monday morning—and Chalk had done the choosing. Miss Queen's real employer was Division Five and her real function was not to assist Paul but to watch him. She was an athletic woman, pleasant yet impersonal, who appeared more capable of flipping her boss over her shoulder than of flipping for him.

Chalk himself was only a few paces across the hall in an office reserved for government inspectors. Since Keller Corp's most recent contract, pre-SWORD, had been to manufacture components for a diving bell, "U.S. Coast Guard" was still painted on the door. Chalk didn't bother to have it changed.

Paul's own door had been freshly painted to identify the new occupant, however. The spacious office occupied the southeast corner of the executive level and overlooked the parking lot. The desk alone was nearly as large as his office at the *Dispatch*. A man could imagine himself a king in the throne-like swivel chair . . . but Paul recalled that the last monarch had found it a death trap.

"Glad you like it," Hank told him. "Take a last look at that clean desk. It'll never be that empty again. I intend to work your tail off, brother-in-law dear."

The jest contained considerable truth. Hank was eager to rid himself of the managerial duties he found tedious. The Pentagon was calling him back to Washington for another conference. He had delayed departure to acquaint Paul with his new responsibilities.

They were many and various. Although Keller Corp was working on several contracts simultaneously—helicopter gun mounts for the Air Force, spacecraft antennae for NASA, plus experimental projects for which no contracts had been let—SWORD was by far the largest. It already engaged three-quarters of the work force. Once full production was underway, that number would swell to nearly one hundred per cent. So while Paul's official title was SWORD Project Manager, he came close to being in charge of the entire plant. Engineering, purchasing, fabrication, assembly, quality control, even the lunchroom . . . all looked to his office for the final decision.

He began with a tour of his seven-acre suzerainty. The factory was a rambling structure of various heights and architectural styles, ugly but functional. It was constantly under expansion as new projects demanded new facilities —in ten years the original plant had tripled in size—until it was no longer one building but several which shared a common roof. Since growth had been haphazard, so was the arrangement, creating a maze of rooms huge and small in which a stranger might easily lose himself.

To make sure that this fate did not befall this latest stranger, Hank appointed himself Paul's guide. Together, they poked into every cavern and cubbyhole, from the windowless drafting room where each project was conceived, through the assembly line which shaped it, to the vast open yard where the finished product was stored for shipment. Paul was shown tools ranging from tiny electron welders to thermal fabricators the size of a family garage. Hank explained the function of each, often in language he had difficulty following. "Don't worry if you don't understand it," Hank reassured him. "Probably isn't one man here who understands it all—including me."

Paul doubted the disclaimer. Keller Corp was Hank's child; he knew it perhaps better than he knew his flesh-and-blood children and loved it only slightly less. That love was extended to his over two hundred employees, all of whom he called by their first names. It was a common joke—and the despair of his secretary—that Hank Keller could not walk through the plant in less than half an hour since he invariably stopped every few paces to discuss a personal problem, extend congratulations on a birth or sympathy on a death, or simply to chat.

"They're good people," he explained a shade defensively when their tour had been interrupted for perhaps the dozenth time. "Did you know that we've got the smallest employee turnover of any firm on the mesa? And damn little union trouble, either. I think that's because my people trust me and I trust them." He grimaced. "Maybe that's why Vandamm was able to pull the wool over my eyes. I couldn't believe that any man who worked here would sell me out. Damn it, I still can't believe it!"

"Maybe Vandamm didn't want to sell you out," Paul suggested. He might not understand engineering techniques as well as Hank, but he knew the human soul far better. "Could be that's why he killed himself instead."

Hank was unconvinced. "He could have come to me. That's what you or I would have done, isn't it? I can't tell you what a relief it is to have you with me, a man I know I can count on."

Hank's special pride and joy was the research division, since he was an inventor at heart, rather than a manufacturer. Paul was surprised to discover that its current work was of a nonmilitary nature, the use of plastics and fiberglass to replace wood as a building material.

"This is the wave of the future for Keller Corp—or so I hope," Hank told him. "I'm looking forward to the day when we can get out of the military hardware business altogether. I want to build a better world, not help destroy it. Look at this stuff, Paul. We can construct a whole house of it, from foundation to shingles, better and safer and even cheaper than with conventional materials. We can lead the way for an entire new industry and I'm as excited as hell about it."

He even viewed SWORD as potentially more valuable for peace than for war, enabling men to map the ocean floor, chart its current and locate its riches. Paul caught some of his vision. He found himself growing excited about helping bring it to reality . . . until he remembered his own reality.

Chalk was a constant reminder. At first, he kept a polite distance and left Paul's surveillance to Miss Queen. However, once Hank had flown off to Washington and doors could be closed without fear of the boss bursting through them unannounced, Chalk got down to business.

"Time we had a talk," he announced, seating himself across the desk which—true to Hank's prediction—was already piled high with papers. "What have you got to report?"

"Bob took the bait. He thinks I'm working for him again."

"Figured he did," Chalk grunted. "Seeing as how you're still breathing." He listened with interest to Paul's sketchy account of how the bargain had been consummated. "So far, so good. I was hoping you'd gotten next to Barnes himself, though."

"I made a strong pitch for dealing with him personally. I don't know whether he'll go for it."

"He'd better. Barnes is the cookie I want. The rest are only crumbs." Chalk had spent the interval in research. The evidence suggested that Bob Barnes might be Innokenty Zubov, a colonel in the First Chief Directorate. Division 5 suspected that Zubov was currently the KGB's chief agent in the United States, a post once held by another colonel, Rudolf Abel. If true, he would be a prize catch indeed—and Chalk plainly hungered to be his captor. He admitted that seizing Zubov would not cripple the enemy for long; a new agent would inevitably replace him. However, victories in this silent war were temporary at best.

Paul's role was to lure Barnes (he could not think of his former mentor by any other name) into the open. And then?

Chalk's reply was a shrug. "You've been on borrowed time for years. Maybe if you're lucky, you'll be able to borrow some more."

Scarcely a reassuring answer but, when you came right down to it, it was all anyone could really expect. Paul was forced to practice what most men merely preached: live each day at a time. For the moment, that wasn't too difficult. Chalk's instructions were identical to those he had received from Barnes, i.e., lead a normal existence. "They'll be suspicious if you come back to them too fast. They'll expect you to learn the routine here first. Go ahead and learn it. Take a week or so before you make your move."

And so Paul worked hard to master a job which he knew he could not keep and to appear cheerful about it, besides. It was more difficult to maintain the pose with Sibby, yet he managed that also. He was less successful in controlling his subconscious. Time after time, he sweated through a recurrent nightmare: He was in a car hurtling down an empty freeway at a fantastic speed toward an inevitable crash. He always awoke before it occurred, and though he told himself that it was only a dream, he knew better.

The plans and specifications for SWORD ran to twenty-five pages, unbound and color-coded. Of these, seventeen were known as the Green Sheets and dealt with the less sensitive portions of the new sonar device. The remaining eight pages—the Red Sheets—detailed the vital heart of the mechanism. Both sets were stamped top secret, but only the latter really deserved the classification. At least a dozen persons, including the late Victor Vandamm, had worked on the Green Sheets; they were passed about casually from department to department with but token supervision. The Red Sheets, however, were guarded jealously and distributed piecemeal on a strict need-to-know basis; only Hank Keller himself was intimately acquainted with all eight. The Green Sheets alone were of little value and it was these that Chalk intended to furnish to the enemy. Since it was a virtual certainty that this information was already in the KGB's possession via Vandamm, duplication would serve to establish Paul's good faith without compromising security. Photocopies were run off and concealed in the lining of the attaché case which he carried to and from the plant each day.

The classified ad appeared in the Wednesday editions of the Los Angeles newspapers. There was no immediate response. The enemy's silence bothered Chalk more than it bothered Paul. He prowled the executive level like a prospective father pacing a maternity waiting room, examined each piece of mail and monitored every phone call. Since patience was the name of the game, Paul wondered at the veteran agent's puzzling lack of it. Miss Queen, in a rare moment of talkativeness, confided the reason. "Joe's had a run of bad luck recently, and he's not getting any younger. Some people feel he may be over the hill. Nailing Barnes has become a personal thing to him, like it's his last chance to prove he's as good as he ever was."

"What happens if this blows up in his face? It could, you know."

"Better hope it doesn't. Joe isn't what you'd call a good loser."

Paul got the message. His alliance with Chalk was an uneasy one at best, with scant love lost on either side. Should the mission on which Chalk was staking his reputation prove to be a fiasco, Paul was the logical scapegoat. The bargain they had struck hinged on success; failure canceled all bets.

It was thirty-six hours after initial publication of the personal notice before Barnes replied. Paul was driving a Keller Corp car since the Econoline van had remained with the *Dispatch*. When he went to the parking lot at quitting time, he found an advertising flyer tucked under the windshield wiper. The flyer offered him a free gift—a set of four plastic tumblers, unbreakable and dishwasher-proof—if he would fill his tank at Mesa Richfield. Similar papers fluttered on nearby windshields; some lay discarded on the asphalt. Paul, who did not need plastic tumblers or buy his own gasoline, folded the flyer and placed it in his pocket. Penciled at the bottom, like a signature, were the two small barns.

Mesa Richfield lay a mile west of the plant on the road to town. Since it shared an intersection with three other stations, each offering identical merchandise at identical prices, business was not especially brisk for any of them. The teen-age attendant rushed out to greet him as if fearing that any delay might send him to one of his competitors. Paul ordered gasoline and presented the flyer. The young man added it to the stack of those already redeemed without a glance at the tiny sketch which made it unique. This, as well as his youth, seemed to rule him out as part of the KGB apparatus. Yet there seemed to be no one else about.

"All alone tonight?" Paul inquired.

"Boss is out to dinner. Shall I check under the hood?"

"Might as well. No—on second thought, forget it."

A man had come around the corner of the station from the direction of the restrooms. He paused to take a drink of water, wiped his mouth with his handkerchief and then, as though discovering Paul for the first time, sauntered toward him. "Going into town?" he asked. "I wonder if you'd mind giving me a ride. I seem to have missed my bus." It was Nylec, the KGB disposal man.

Paul hesitated. Had Barnes discovered the deception and sent Nylec to settle the score? It seemed an unnecessarily involved method of murder. In any case, he had little choice except to play along. "Sure. Hop in."

The signal flashed orange as they turned out of the station driveway. "Run it," Nylec ordered tersely. They shot across the intersection against the red light to the accompaniment of indignant horns and unheard curses from opposing motorists. Nylec looked pleased with the maneuver which served to block off a trailing vehicle, or at least render it immediately obvious. "Straight ahead."

"Where's Bob? I've got to talk with him."

Nylec didn't reply. He drew a metal box the size of a small transistor radio from his pocket and placed it on the console between them. A twist of the dial brought forth a high-frequency whine calculated to jam reception on all but the most sophisticated listening devices; it was known familiarly as the "bug killer." His precautions taken, he said, "Next right."

A two-lane road branched off the highway, dipping into a canyon. Once it had been a favorite short cut to the beach. Now, with the coming of the freeway, it was little traveled. They descended through the winding gully at a reduced speed made necessary by the rutted asphalt and into a valley, past an abandoned fruit stand and an

167

equally quiet pet cemetery. Nylec pointed ahead. "See those trees? Pull up there."

A grove of eucalyptus grew on each side of the road, rearing up like giants among the low chaparral and scrub oak. The tall trees, planted in orderly rows, were a common sight throughout Southern California. They had been imported from Australia a half-century earlier in an ill-fated attempt to grow low-cost timber. Long since abandoned, they served no purpose except to provide shade for picnickers and a nest for birds. They also could serve as an ideal spot for an execution, Paul realized uneasily; a body might lie undiscovered under the thick carpet of leaves for weeks. He was relieved to discover another automobile parked there. It contained a single occupant, a man.

"Don't turn off your motor," Nylec commanded. He was out of the car before it had come to a full halt. The driver of the other vehicle, moving with the same alacrity, took his place beside Paul. The switch was accomplished with the speed and precision of a Pony Express relay.

"Let's go," the newcomer said. He gave Paul a comradely slap on the shoulder. "Well, Eddie—here we are again."

"I knew it had to be you," Paul said slowly. "But I wasn't really sure until you spoke. You've changed a lot."

"Partly my choice, partly nature's," Bob Barnes agreed with a chuckle. "More the latter than the former, I'm afraid." His body was as lithe as ever, but the black hair was nearly gone and what remained was flecked with gray, as was the neat beard. Hornrim glasses masked the sharp eyes which, Paul noted, were brown now rather than blue. "You've changed a bit yourself, Eddie."

"Not enough, I guess. You were able to recognize me."

"The voice again," Barnes explained. "You can cut

your hair or wear a wig. You can grow a beard or shave one off. You can even change the color of your eyes with contacts. But a voice is nearly as unique as a fingerprint. When I saw your photograph, I was struck by the resemblance to my late lamented friend and associate. Yet even after my investigation demonstrated that Paul Towers *could* be Eddie Young, I still wondered if it wasn't simply a startling case of look-alikes. But when I matched your voice print with the one in your old dossier . . ."

"Not that it matters, but how'd you get my voice print?"

"Over the phone. Have you forgotten the cheerful chap who called you a few weeks back to congratulate you on winning a valuable gift? You were rather rude to me, in fact."

Paul remembered the call, less for its content than for its inopportune timing. He remembered also that he had requested Sibby not to interrupt their lovemaking to answer the telephone. It wouldn't have made any difference in the long run, since Barnes would have persisted. Yet it was ironic to realize that he had unwittingly marked himself for death while engaged in that most life-expressing of human activities.

"Why did you try to kill me, Bob? I wasn't doing you any harm. And we were friends once."

"Men like me have no friends. It's a luxury we can't afford. I'll admit I was fonder of you than most. Ordering your removal wasn't an easy decision. But we were bound to run into each other sooner or later in a community as small as Orchestra Beach. I couldn't risk jeopardizing my mission."

"You can't imagine how much better I feel to hear that it wasn't anything personal."

Barnes acknowledged the sarcasm with a smile. "I'm delighted that the situation now offers me another option. An amazing coincidence, though, that you of all people should be Victor Vandamm's replacement."

"It wasn't a coincidence at all. Hank offered me the job and I'd decided to turn it down. When I found out you were stalking me, I figured I'd better get something to bargain with and get it fast."

"That jibes with my information," Barnes agreed without revealing where the information had come from. "Even so, some of my associates believe I'm making a mistake to accept you."

"Who besides Nylec?"

"I certainly don't mean Alice," Barnes parried. "You do have a marvelous knack with women, Eddie. Not many men are able to find even one wife who will love them so deeply. You seem to have found two. What's your secret?"

"Just lucky, I guess."

"I'm not sure it's a blessing. Love creates obligations, and obligations create problems. We tried to teach you back in Middletown to use women without becoming involved with them. I'm afraid that's one subject you flunked. Which is the reason you're in a bind now. I'd have cut and run the moment I discovered my life was in danger. But you stayed—because of the charming Sybil, right?"

Paul was disturbed to learn that the other man was still able to read him so accurately. "I assumed we were going to talk business, not about my love life."

"The two can't always be separated." Barnes shrugged. "All right, let's talk business. What do you have for me?"

"The attaché case, under the lining."

Barnes used a pocket knife to pry up the false bottom. He removed the photocopies and riffled through them quickly. "Where are the rest of them?"

"That's all I've been able to get. At least, it's a beginning."

"I disagree. It isn't a beginning. It isn't anything at all." He tossed the photocopies contemptuously back into the attaché case. "I had this much from Vandamm weeks ago."

"How the hell was I supposed to know?" Paul snapped; a little righteous indignation seemed appropriate. "I've been operating in the dark. If you'd met me when I first wanted you to instead of hiding behind women and disposal men—"

"Calm down," Barnes advised with a chuckle. "I guess we're both a bit uptight. But you must have known that it's the Red Sheets I really want."

"Sure, I knew that. What I didn't know was how to get them. The Red Sheets are locked up real good. Joe Chalk watches them—and me—like a hawk."

"Do you think Chalk suspects you?"

"No. But he doesn't trust me, either. Hell, Chalk doesn't even trust his own mother, if he has one. He practically sleeps with those damn plans."

"I'm disappointed in you, Eddie. I consider you more than a match for Chalk." He was professionally scornful of the Division 5 field supervisor and, indeed, of Division 5 itself, which he rated as inferior to the British and French intelligence services, about on a par with the West Germans—and, of course, not even in the same league with his own. "They do labor under a handicap," he conceded. "They lack the confidence and respect of their own countrymen. The ridiculous conceit that there's something un-American about espionage . . . it's no wonder that their agents are a second-rate lot."

"Chalk did smoke out Vandamm," Paul reminded him.

"But too late, as usual. And Victor was an amateur, not

really one of us. You and I together, we'll handle Chalk, all right. Tell me what steps he's taken to protect the Red Sheets."

Paul complied in detail. When he finished, Barnes clucked his tongue thoughtfully. "Basically the same as during Victor's tenure except for the addition of Miss Queen. Good. That confirms my feeling that Chalk is a man without much imagination. He substitutes routine, always a mistake because it breeds a false sense of security. As any good bank robber will confirm. Run over the daily schedule again, please."

"Chalk and I—and sometimes Hank, if he's around— take the Red Sheets out of the vault every morning at nine. No earlier because of the time lock. They go directly to my office, never anywhere else. If Engineering or Drafting or Purchasing need to refer to them, they do it there. Either Chalk or Miss Queen or both have their eyes on them every minute. At noon, the Red Sheets usually go back to the vault—"

"Usually?"

"Sometimes the work isn't finished by noon and rather than return the sheets to the vault and reset the timer and then get them out again, we simply hold them during lunchtime. When that happens, Chalk and Miss Queen spell each other standing guard while the other one goes to the lunchroom."

Barnes squinted absently out the window. They were on the outskirts of town, passing an elementary school playground where a group of youngsters were holding an impromptu Olympics. The one hundred yard dash was just beginning. "How long do you estimate it would take Chalk to run from the lunchroom to your office?"

"I've never seen Chalk run. I could cover the distance in three minutes, maybe four."

Barnes appeared to change the subject, but Paul knew he hadn't, really. "You were trained in microphotography, weren't you? Of course you were—operation of the S2 camera was a requirement at Middletown. So if I could arrange for you to have those three minutes, maybe four, alone with the Red Sheets, you'd have ample time to photograph them, wouldn't you?"

"You're forgetting Miss Queen."

"On the contrary. My thought is to create a diversion. Since Miss Queen is presumably the weaker vessel, I feel it should be aimed at her. Fill me in on her, Eddie. You can skip the physical description—I already know that—but what is she like as a person? Tastes and aversions, foibles, vanities, that sort of thing."

"When I think of Miss Queen, the color gray comes to mind automatically. She doesn't seem to have any of the ordinary feminine quirks. She's not married, never mentions her family, apparently doesn't have any love life. No pets, either. She doesn't even make the usual trips to the powder room to put on fresh lipstick, because she doesn't wear any. The only thing that turns her on is her car. It's a Porsche 911S, a real beauty. She talks about that car the way most women talk about their kids."

"The maternal instinct," Barnes murmured. "Sublimate it how you may. I suggest you buy a philodendron for your office, a good-sized one. The next time that Chalk goes to lunch and leaves the Red Sheets in Miss Queen's tender care, place the plant on your windowsill. To get a little sun, if she asks. That will be the signal for me to attempt to lure her out of the way for those precious three minutes. I'm not sure yet how I'll do it—that needs a bit more thought—but you're to be ready to move when it happens. I'll arrange to supply you with the S2 camera. If the scheme works, remove the philodendron from your window. You'll be contacted with instructions on where to meet me. How does that sound to you?"

"Risky."

"Certainly. Ours is a high-risk occupation. You haven't let middle-class living make you soft, have you? I can set up this operation—but you're going to have to carry it off. If you've lost your nerve . . ."

Paul met the probing gaze. "You furnish the diversion. I'll furnish the nerve."

"Good boy." Barnes squeezed his arm affectionately. "Almost like old times," he said. "I'm really delighted to be working with you again, Eddie."

Paul nearly found himself reciprocating the sentiment. Against all logic, still he felt as in the past strongly drawn to the other man. Ironically, Barnes his enemy was a far more attractive personality than Chalk his ally. For one fleeting instant he was attempted to shuck his role as the Judas goat leading Barnes to the slaughter. Then he remembered that the role had been forced upon him and that Barnes, after all, had done the forcing. Since he could not avoid the shambles that lay ahead, better to play the treacherous goat than the doomed sheep.

Barnes didn't appear to notice his silence. "Yes," he continued, "I was actually quite broken up when it appeared you'd gone down with that airliner. How did you manage to arrange that, by the way?"

"I missed my flight. A piece of blind luck."

"I supposed it had to be something of the sort. You're not the type who could arrange a deliberate accident. You always were too tender-hearted, Eddie. That can be a fatal flaw in our profession."

"Well, nobody's perfect."

Barnes smiled. He deactivated the bug killer and they

drove the rest of the way without speaking further. Paul dropped him off in the center of the Orchestra Beach business district. As he drove away, Paul saw that the KGB's top agent was buying a statuette of Tihoya at a sidewalk souvenir stand. He wondered if Barnes knew that he had posed for the figure—and, if so, whether there was a significance to his purchase.

Chalk's reaction was mixed. On the one hand, he was satisfied that things were going well. On the other, he was disappointed that they hadn't gone better. The revised description of Barnes was of little more help in identifying him than the old one had been. Thanks to the Fiesta, the town overflowed with bearded men. Nor could they be confident that the hair was genuine, anyway. Since Barnes had falsified the color of his eyes, the balance of his appearance might be equally spurious. "I wish you'd tipped me off ahead of time that you were going to meet him," Chalk grumbled. "I could have put a tail on him, see where he went."

"Thank God I didn't. You're not dealing with an amateur, man! You'd have blown it sure."

"No way," Chalk scoffed. "Christ almighty, don't you think I know my business?"

Paul let it pass. While not doubting Chalk's experience, he feared that Miss Queen was right and time had caught up with the veteran. It happened to every man eventually. An athlete lost his reflexes; an agent lost his judgment. He began to press, to take unnecessary risks. In espionage as in poker, the pot generally went to the player who kept his cool. "Bob's by way of being a genius at his trade," he explained. "He can see around corners and through walls. And what he can't see he can sense."

Chalk remained unimpressed. "Pardon me all to hell if I don't buy the Superman bit. Just because he psychs women and kids don't mean that he psychs me."

Later the same day Paul was visited by a salesman whose ostensible purpose was to interest Keller Corp in a prepaid medical and hospitalization plan for its employees. Since the company already subscribed to Blue Cross, Paul brushed him off. The salesman, cordial to the last, insisted on leaving with him a brochure which Paul promptly put into the wastebasket and a cigarette lighter, bearing an advertising message, which he put on his desk.

Hank saw it there and would have claimed it for himself. "You're too late," Paul told him. "I've already promised it to Joe." He had recognized the gift for what it was, the vehicle which concealed the S2 microfilm camera.

Chalk, who had a fondness for gadgetry, was intrigued with the device whose bottom slid aside to reveal a tiny lens. Paul requested him nervously not to fool with it. "The thing's booby-trapped. An explosive wire. Try to take it apart without knowing how and it'll blow up in your face."

"How do we deactivate it?"

"I don't know. I was never cleared on the assembly, just on the operation."

"How come? Don't the Reds trust their own people?"

Paul refused to be drawn into an argument. "Well, it's a pretty sophisticated instrument. Holds enough film to photograph an average-size newspaper—and in a bad light, too." He grinned. "On top of that, the lighter works every time."

When relations are strained, even a pleasantry can be misunderstood. Chalk chose to interpret it as a boast of Soviet technical superiority. So the day ended as it had begun, in an atmosphere of mutual hostility. Paul carried

his vile humor home with him. He was only partly mollified to discover a better-than-average dinner awaiting him
and the cook costumed in sleek hostess pajamas usually reserved for entertaining company. The table was set for
only two, however. "Okay," he asked suspiciously, "what're
you up to?"

"I don't know what you mean, darling," Sibby trilled,
falsely innocent.

"Candlelight, wine, those pajamas and that sexy per-
fume . . . There's got to be an ulterior motive."

She grinned sheepishly. "You know me too darn well.
The truth is that I have an announcement to make and I
wanted you to be in a good mood."

"Announcement?" He regarded her sharply. "My God
—you're not!"

"What? Oh, no—of course, I'm not. Though I must say
I don't care for that horrified reaction. Would it be so terrible if I were pregnant?"

"I didn't mean it the way it sounded," he alibied, although he could scarcely imagine a more unwelcome de-
velopment at this particular moment. "It's just that,
well—"

"I know," she said tartly. "You're not ready yet. When
will you be ready, I wonder?" Without waiting for an answer, she went on, "Well, my announcement isn't that
earth-shaking. In fact, it's so trivial that now I don't think
I'll even bother you with it."

This was an invitation for him to coax her into revealing the secret. Much as he didn't feel like it, he complied;
to do otherwise would cause hurt feelings. Sibby allowed
herself to be persuaded. Her news was that, although the
class at IBS was concluding, Shevlin had invited her to assist him in some experimental work involving extrasensory perception. "I'm the only one he asked," she said

proudly. "Except Mrs. Urich, and she already works for him. Some of the other gals from Personal Potential are ready to claw my eyes out, no fooling. Isn't it exciting? I told Larry I'd have to ask your permission first—but I didn't think you'd have any objections."

"Think again. I don't care to have a wife who's able to read my mind."

He was more than halfway serious, but she chose to interpret it as a joke. "Scared I'll uncover all your secrets, huh? Well, you don't have to worry. ESP isn't really mind reading. I mean, it is and it isn't. Larry claims that thought transference may be possible under the right conditions but only when both parties cooperate."

Paul conquered his uneasiness. After all, it was she not he who had been invited to participate in the experiments and it was he not she who had something to conceal. Nor could he in justice allow his jitters to cancel out her innocent pleasure. "Okay. But I warn you—the first time I catch you trying to read my mind, it's all over. Now that I've said yes, do I still get the full treatment?"

"The full treatment," she murmured, giving him a lingering kiss. "Now or later, darling?"

"There you go already. How'd you know what I meant?"

Sibby chuckled. "That isn't ESP. Or if it is, every wife has it without any special training."

On his way to work the following morning Paul bought a split leaf philodendron in a gallon-sized clay pot and a black wrought-iron stand on which to place it. He installed the plant in a corner of his office adjacent to the window which overlooked the parking lot. It was his only accomplishment of the day. Chalk didn't show up for work—Miss Queen would say merely that he had been "called away"—and in his absence the Red Sheets remained securely locked in the vault. There were other tasks pursuant to getting SWORD into production but Paul, his mind on a more vital matter, found them wearisome. When Chalk did not appear on the next day either, the nervousness caused by this unexpected delay threatened to overpower him.

"You sure were restless last night," Sibby informed him. "And when I touched you, your skin was positively clammy. I hope you're not coming down with something."

"Too much on my mind, that's all." He managed a weak grin. "I hear there's a lot of that going around."

Chalk returned on the third day with no more warning than when he had disappeared. Paul found him slouched in his office chair—and if Paul had slept badly, Chalk bore the appearance of a man who hadn't slept at all. His chin was unshaven and his eyes red-rimmed, yet he greeted Paul with surprising joviality. "About time you showed up. Grab yourself a cup of coffee."

"Where the hell have you been, anyway?"

"Washington. Flew into L.A. at four this morning and came straight here. Care to snap a few pictures?"

Although it still lacked twenty minutes before nine o'clock, the Red Sheets had already been removed from the vault. The large crimson folder lay atop his desk, the cigarette lighter-camera beside it. He regarded Chalk incredulously. "You're not suggesting that I actually film them, are you?"

"Barnes wants pictures of the Red Sheets. I've decided to give him some."

"For God's sake, why? Blank film will do just as well for bait and he won't know it's blank until it's too late."

"Wrong. I need a strong rope to hang him with. If all Barnes has in his pocket when I arrest him is an empty camera, where's my case? A good lawyer could get it thrown right out of court. But if Barnes has pictures of top-secret documents, that'll fix his wagon for sure."

"And if Bob manages to slip through your fingers, whose wagon gets fixed then?"

"Never thought of that," Chalk muttered. "It would be kind of embarrassing, wouldn't it?" His lips commenced to quiver, his shoulders shook and he gave way to laughter he was unable to control. "Do you think I'm stupid enough to throw him the real Red Sheets, even as bait? Hell, they're back in the vault. Those are fakes—but damn good ones. I've worked on them around the clock the last couple of days, me and a detail from Counterfeiting."

Paul was forced to concede that, familiar as he was with the plans, he could not tell where the real left off and the false began, so skillfully had the formulae and diagrams been altered. The forgeries, which Chalk was pleased to point out, included—as a final touch of authenticity—marginal notes and corrections in the inventor's distinctive scrawl. "I guarantee that they'd fool Hank Keller himself, unless he checked out all the equations. Beautiful, huh? Barnes gets ten-to-twenty for stealing something that isn't worth the paper it's printed on. I want to see his face when he hears that." Chalk wished not only to beat his opponent but to humiliate him as well. That, as much as the need to build an airtight case, was the reason for the elaborate preparations.

Once the spurious Red Sheets were filmed, Chalk fed them into the shredder and burned the fragments. He did so reluctantly; Paul suspected he would have preferred them bronzed as a monument to his ingenuity. But the destruction was necessary lest the duplication be discovered and commented upon. Chalk felt reasonably sure that the

KGB had placed another agent inside Keller Corp. He considered the parking lot attendant the most likely candidate. Several facts fed his suspicion. The attendant, a cheerful chap named Rhoades (and inevitably dubbed Dusty), had been hired on Victor Vandamm's recommendation. More significantly, not only could Dusty have placed the flyer on Paul's car, but he alone of all Keller Corp's employees had a clear and continuous view of Paul's window where the signal for the diversion was to be displayed. Prudently Chalk refrained from digging into Dusty's antecedents for the moment.

"No use shaking the tree until all the fruit's ripe. Once I nab Barnes, we'll pick the tree clean—Dusty, Muse, Oatis and Associates, the whole crew, all at once." He was quietly mobilizing Division 5's manpower, bringing in reinforcements from as far east as Albuquerque. Paul was reminded of two armies girding for battle, each aware of the other's existence but not its strategy, moving inexorably toward the showdown . . . while he occupied the perilous no-man's land between them.

Chalk chose Thursday as the moment to launch his offensive. Like many command decisions, his was influenced more by instinct, a gut feeling that the time was right, than by cold logic. Being human, he found a number of ex post facto reasons to support him, among them that Thursday was Hank Keller's Rotary meeting. Thus, Hank would be absent from the plant during the lunch hour when he otherwise made a habit of dropping in for a chat with SWORD's project manager.

The Red Sheets were removed from the vault at nine o'clock that morning as usual. Paul spent the forenoon with Solly Ambrose, Keller Corp's purchasing agent. Ambrose's problem (which Paul was expected to solve) was that the price of certain metals, notably titanium, used in the construction of SWORD's traveling wave tube, was rumored to increase sharply during the coming quarter. Since the Pentagon had not yet authorized full-scale production, should Keller Corp order only the titanium presently needed—or should they stockpile the metal on the hopeful supposition that it would be needed in the future? (To add a further complicating factor, Research was experimenting with a new plastic which, if it turned out to be all the scientists hoped, would replace their need for titanium altogether.) The gamble involved nearly one hundred thousand dollars, which would need to be borrowed. This in turn created another dilemma. Would the savings effected through buying the titanium now be less than if they waited for a dip in interest rates after the first of the year, another rumor?

Ambrose, who dealt in materiel rather than money, preferred to believe that prices were more likely to go up than interest rates to go down and so favored stockpiling the titanium. (Never mind the miracle plastic; the boys in Research were inveterate optimists.) Paul, conscious of his fiscal responsibility, was inclined to the side of caution. Ordinarily, he would have enjoyed the sharp but amiable argument. This morning he had difficulty concentrating on it. Chalk, the omnipresent silent observer, glanced frequently at his watch, reminding him of the far greater gamble he was engaged in. When the noon whistle sounded, the debate was still unresolved.

"Let's break for chow and take it up again this afternoon," he suggested. "I'd like to bring Hank in on it. After all, he's the one who's going to have to go to the bank if we decide your way, Solly."

"Suits me," Ambrose agreed. "And just to prove that we're still friends, I'll even buy your lunch."

"You sure know how to hurt a guy, don't you? My doctor's put me on a diet. All I'm allowed for lunch is a tall glass of water and a vitamin pill."

"Tell me who your doctor is—so I never make the mistake of going to him. How about you, Joe? Join me for a bite?"

Chalk got to his feet, stretching. "I thought you'd never ask. I'm on no diet—especially if you're buying." He gestured at the Red Sheets on Paul's desk. "Going to be needing them any more?"

Paul pretended to consider. "Maybe you'd better leave them out just in case."

Chalk raised his voice to summon Miss Queen. "Nora, I'm going to eat with Solly. Take over, will you?" He gave Paul a brief significant glance and sauntered after Ambrose's pudgy figure.

Miss Queen took the chair her superior had vacated. She and Paul regarded each other for a moment, then he murmured, "Well, here goes nothing." He removed the philodendron from its stand and placed it on the windowsill.

The signal given, Miss Queen inched forward expectantly. "What do you think is going to happen?"

"I don't know. Maybe nothing. Could be Bob hasn't had enough time to set up the diversion. All we can do is wait."

They waited. A minute passed, then another, finally five. At the end of ten, Miss Queen, unable to sit quietly any longer, began to pace. "Are they or aren't they?" she muttered. Since Paul didn't have the answer, he limited his reply to a shrug. The tense silence continued.

It was broken by the buzz of the telephone. The sound, too soft to wake a sleeping baby, caused them both to jump as if touched by an electric prod. "Take it easy," Paul cautioned, himself as well as his companion. "It may be a false alarm."

It was not. The male voice on the line belonged to Dusty, the parking lot attendant. "Hey, is Miss Queen there? Tell her that smoke's pouring out of her car and I can't open the damn doors. Unless she gets down here fast with the keys the whole thing's likely to burn up."

"Right!" Without covering the mouthpiece, he informed Miss Queen, "Your car's on fire."

"Oh, my God!" She sprang to the window, nearly upsetting the philodendron. Craning over her shoulder, Paul could see smoke boiling out of the scarlet Porsche through the windows which had been left open a crack in deference to the heat. He told Dusty that Miss Queen was on her way and ordered him to notify the plant fire department.

"Wait!" Miss Queen was fumbling in her purse. Stricken by the disaster that had befallen her most prized possession, she had momentarily forgotten all else. "Tell him I'll throw down the keys so he can—"

Paul broke the connection. "You'll take them down there yourself. That's the whole goddam point!" His fierce tone snapped Miss Queen out of her shock, but he still was forced to remind her to instruct the switchboard to page Chalk. As he closed the door behind her fleeing form, the public address system began to blare Chalk's name, summoning him to return to the project manager's office on the double. Paul regarded the Red Sheets glumly. So carefully guarded, yet vulnerable after all; so much for secrets. Barnes, the shrewd student of human behavior, had found the weak spot in the defense. Of course, he'd had Chalk's cooperation—but Paul did not doubt that the ruse would have been equally successful without it.

It took Chalk longer than expected to arrive, a full thirty seconds beyond the maximum time required to photograph the secret documents had that been Paul's real mission. He burst in, panting and limping. The front of his white shirt was sopping wet, but not from perspiration. "Ran into some clown with a bowl of soup," he growled. "Twisted my ankle, too. What happened?"

"See for yourself." Paul made room for him at the window. Together, they watched the frantic efforts of Miss Queen and Dusty to extinguish the blaze, a feat they were unable to accomplish until the plant firemen arrived to smother the Porsche with foam.

"Not bad," Chalk admitted, and he was not referring to the firemen's expertise. "Must have been incendiary jelly with a delayed fuse. A bit gaudy—but it worked."

His grudging admiration for the enemy was not shared by Miss Queen, who returned grimy with smoke and close to tears. The fire had done no structural damage, but it had gutted the Porsche's interior. Although insurance would take care of the cost of repairs, she doubted she would be able to replace the imported vicuna seat covers at any price. And nothing could repay her for the trauma. "Nice friends you have," she told Paul balefully. "Oh, how I'd love to get my hands on that bastard!"

"Then why don't we invite the bastard to drop around? Pardon me." Paul removed the philodendron from the window. "I think we've all had enough heat for one day."

Barnes accepted the invitation with alacrity. In the mail the following morning Paul received a cordial, albeit form, letter from The Date Bureau, a newly opened establishment modeled in the swinging image of the successful Playboy Clubs. The letter informed him that he, as a rising young executive (and, presumably, a swinger also), had been selected to receive a free trial membership. A one-time-only guest card was enclosed. Paul would have dismissed it as a routine promotional gimmick. However, penciled on the guest card was a specific date, today's, and an hour, nine p.m.

Chalk agreed that the rendezvous was well-chosen from Barnes' point of view. The Date Bureau was bound to be crowded on a Friday evening, the beginning of the weekend, and a dictum of the espionage service held that private business was best conducted in a public place. Since admission to the club was restricted, all who entered could be scrutinized, ruling out the possibility that Division 5 operatives might mingle with the throng unnoticed. Even if they were able to obtain guest cards at this late date, their identities were presumably known to the enemy. Nor could they attempt to infiltrate the staff on such short notice. It seemed unlikely that The Date Bureau was a KGB front operation. On the other hand, an agent among the employees was a distinct possibility. A number of the scientist types from the defense firms on the mesa (Keller Corp included) were known to frequent the club. Thus, it made an ideal listening post to pick up a secret or two, plus information on sexual indiscretions for the purpose of blackmail.

His options limited, Chalk chose the best of those open to him. He planned to spread his net around The Date Bureau, staking out all exits in order to arrest Barnes as he left the club with the incriminating film in his possession. A circumspect investigation of the premises indicated that this wasn't going to be easy, either. The Date Bureau occupied an upper story of a new office building adjacent to the shopping center north of town. Yet it was far from being a trap; Chalk was able to count at least eight exits from the club itself . . . plus an equal number from the

Royal Surf Motel to whose top floor it was connected by an above-the-street moving sidewalk.

"I can cover them all, I guess," Chalk mused, "but it's going to spread me mighty damn thin. And that's no good. We've got to grab Barnes fast, swarm all over him, not give him a chance to use the destruct mechanism on the camera. But if we don't know which way he's coming out . . ."

"Put a man on the phone downstairs," Paul suggested. "When Bob leaves, I'll clue you on the route he's taking."

"Right idea, wrong instrument. I've had bad experiences with pay phones in the past. Either it's out of order or you lose your dime or some drunk will have it tied up just when you need it. You can use this instead."

"This" was a miniaturized walkie-talkie no larger than a woman's compact. "The range is limited, but it'll handle this job. All you have to do is push the button and say 'main elevator' or 'the stairs' or whatever and I'll have a half-dozen men there to jump on Barnes. He'll think he ran into the Rams' front four."

He was exhilarated at the prospect of victory, now only a few hours away. Paul, however, wondered about victory's aftermath. "What happens to me then? Bob will know immediately that I sold him out."

"No doubt—but he won't be able to do a damn thing about it. The minute I get Barnes, I'm moving against his whole apparatus. You'll be safe enough. I may need your evidence, but I can arrange for you to testify behind closed doors."

"There's bound to be rumors just the same. People are going to wonder why I left Keller Corp so suddenly. Or am I mistaken in believing that this is my last day as SWORD project manager?"

Chalk shrugged. "It was only a temporary arrangement

and you knew it. I can't allow you to go on handling sensitive material indefinitely. Sure, there'll be questions asked—but you don't have to answer them."

"It's obvious you've never been married."

"Oh, you can tell your wife that the reason you took the job was to help me crack the nasty old spy ring. Now that you've done that, you're quitting because you never really dug the work, anyway. Or think up your own excuse."

"Another lie," Paul said gloomily. "I was hoping I wouldn't have to tell her any more."

"Funny thing about lies. Once you start, it's hard as hell to quit. At least you're improving. Now you're up to telling half-truths."

The distinction was dubious since truth, like virginity, is an absolute. In any case, the end of deceit was not yet in sight. He telephoned Sibby not to expect him home for dinner because he would be (what else?) working late at the office.

Sibby reacted with chagrin. "One of the things I liked best about your new job was that you'd be able to keep regular hours," she reminded him.

"Maybe I should quit," he suggested to see what she'd say.

What she said was: "Don't you dare! But I do intend to have a sisterly talk with Hank and warn him not to work you so hard. Just because Marilyn is willing to put up with an absentee husband is no reason I have to." She added jokingly, "Besides, I remember all the trouble you got into the last time you decided to work late. Don't you?"

He did; it was the night Fred Rossi had died in his stead. "Don't worry. I promise to be very, very careful." That, at least, was the solid unvarnished copper-bottomed gold-plated truth.

The Date Bureau was a sybaritic establishment which catered to the single man and single woman (although no proof of marital status was demanded) and whose function it was to provide an attractive and uninhibited setting where the twain might meet. Designating it as a private club imparted a certain rakish respectability and enabled management to bar homosexuals, voyeurs and minors. High prices kept out a fourth class, equally undesirable, the small spenders. The Date Bureau was not a restaurant, although there was a build-your-own-sandwich counter—ostensibly free, but the ten-dollar cover charge permitted such small generosities. It was not a cocktail lounge, although there were two bars, well-stocked, and a dozen pert barmaids, well-stacked. It was not a night club either, although there was a tiny dance floor, a rock band and occasional impromptu entertainment drawn from among the membership. It was, in sum, a temple consecrated to hedonistic pleasures where the sole commandment was: Thou Shalt Not Bug Thy Neighbors. The aura was deliberately carnal, from the scantily clad waitresses to the priapic murals, intended to instill a feeling of what-the-hell-anything-goes-here. It wasn't quite true; friendships might be born at the club but were required to flower elsewhere. Frequently this was no farther removed than the motel across the street, discreetly reached by the moving sidewalk, where rooms were usually available and registration always easy. A generation earlier, The Date Bureau would have been considered a scandal by the citizenry, denounced from the pulpit and closed by the authorities. In these more permissive days, it was viewed with amused toleration. Everyone's supposed to be free to do his own thing, isn't he? Get with it, man!

Paul arrived a few minutes before nine. He surrendered his guest card to a hostess in a transparent blouse (did he really see what he thought he saw?) and was passed along to the maitre d', a raffish young man who wore a turtleneck sweater rather than a tuxedo. He shrugged when Paul mentioned that he expected to be joined shortly by a friend. "So who doesn't? *Sol o sombra, amigo?*" At Paul's blank look, the maitre d' explained patiently that the phrase—sun or shade?—borrowed from the lexicon of the Spanish bull ring was meant to inquire his preference in the matter of a table. Did Paul wish to be secluded (*sombra*) or in the center of things (*sol*)? Paul chose the latter in order to make his presence obvious.

The dim spacious room was already filled nearly to capacity with the thank-God-it's-Friday crowd. Paul was led to an empty table adjacent to the dance floor. It was conspicuous enough but put him in uncomfortable proximity to the band who, with more hair than talent, seemed to confuse noise with music. A barmaid in the briefest of mini skirts appeared magically at his elbow to take his shouted order for a vodka collins. Her name, she informed him throatily, was Darlene; her pleasure was to serve him "in any way I can." The coquetry was meant merely to establish the sensual mood. As far as the employees were concerned, the unwritten law was: Look, Don't Touch.

Paul looked, not only at Darlene but at his fellow sybarites. There were nearly as many women present as men, a wry tribute to the emancipation of their sex, which permitted them to be the hunters as well as the hunted. He was surprised to discover that the median age of the group was over thirty, rather than younger, as he would have supposed. Most sat alone, like himself. It was still early in the evening. Later, when the liquor and the primitive pulse of the music made them sufficiently bold, they would form liaisons. At the moment hopeful expectation prevailed and their eyes, roving constantly, asked the question: Are you the one?

Paul's eyes roved on a different quest. He did not see the special one he sought at any of the other tables. There were fifty in all, numbered in blue neon (his was Table 12) and each outfitted with a telephone. The member was able to phone any other table in the room (but not outside), simply by dialing the proper number. Thus, if you spied a prospective partner, you could call and make your pitch without leaving your chair. This method avoided embarrassment for both sides, since the pickups were rendered less obvious and so were the refusals. Women initiated fully as many of the calls as the men. However, some remnants of the double standard remained. If agreement was reached, the man joined the woman at her table, rather than vice versa. Should he choose to remain, the tab also became the male responsibility. As a result, table hopping was frequent and in some cases rapid.

Paul waited, ignoring the appraising glances cast in his direction. His telephone rang twice, anyway; both times he pleaded a prior claim. At nine-thirty the maitre d', seeing him still alone, inquired pointedly if everything was to his satisfaction. There was scant profit to be made from singletons who insisted on remaining single. Paul assured him that his companion for the evening would arrive momentarily and placated him—and the archly seductive Darlene—by ordering another highball. He drank this one more rapidly. Where was Barnes, anyway?

His telephone buzzed for the third time. He answered with an annoyance he made no effort to disguise. "You look lonely," a female voice cooed in his ear. "I'm lonely, too. Any reason we can't be lonely together?"

"Not a reason in the world," Paul said slowly. "You sound like just my type."

Barnes chuckled. "Table 44, Eddie. In the far corner, behind you."

He had scrutinized every man entering the room during the past three-quarters of an hour, yet he had failed to recognize Barnes. When he reached Table 44, Paul discovered why. Its occupant was not a man but a woman, a striking brunette who looked to be about thirty-five, smartly gowned and wearing perhaps a shade too much make-up. Paul stared at her for a moment, then sat down. "You're absolutely stunning, my dear."

Barnes' crimson mouth smiled, the false eyelashes fluttered. "I've always rather fancied myself in drag, actually. Tonight it was a necessity, of course. The club rules prohibit two men occupying the same table." He continued to maintain the feminine role with posture and gestures but not in voice. The blaring music served to make conversation unintelligible to the nearest table. "Well, Eddie, how are you *'sta sera?*"

"Jumpy as hell," Paul confessed to explain the nervousness he could not hide. "I feel like I've been waiting here only slightly less than forever."

"Sorry about that. I had to make some last-minute arrangements. Not to mention that it takes hours to get into this outfit. What women go through! No wonder they're always late."

"Do you mind if we skip the small talk, Bob? I'd like to get this thing over with."

Barnes extracted a pack of cigarettes from his purse. "Could I trouble you for a light?" Paul obliged and left the lighter sitting on the table between them. Barnes appeared to be in no hurry to appropriate it. "Behold," he mused. "The fruit of our labors, the end product of all that planning and agony and God knows how many man hours. I suppose I should feel like cheering."

"Don't you?"

"I feel more like weeping. That we should sweat and

bleed and die for so very little, perhaps for nothing whatever." His painted mouth quirked. "For all any of us know, our own Soviet scientists may be working right now on a device identical to SWORD. They may even be farther along with it than Hank Keller. Which would make everything I've done to get that film—and everything Chalk has done to prevent me—so much wasted effort, wouldn't it? It's happened before, certainly, many times. And will again, without a doubt."

"If you know that, how can you be a party to it? It's so damn insane, Bob! That's why I had to get out."

"Oh, I recognize the insanity. Sometimes, like now, I even deplore it. But I accept insanity as the normal condition of mankind. Why fight it? The world enjoys its illness. It stamps out any fool who tries to cure it. You remember the old saying: When you live with a cripple, you learn how to limp. The choice isn't between getting out and staying in, as you seem to believe. The choice is between learning to limp—or perishing. And, if you wish to do more than merely survive, you learn how to limp better than your fellow cripples. I tried to tell you that years ago. Too bad you didn't listen to me."

Before Paul could reply, a hand slapped him on the back and a gay voice cried, "Well, I'll be damned! Paul, baby!" He turned, startled, and saw George Dickman grinning down at him. "What in the hell are a couple of nice kids like you doing in a place like . . ." The rest of the sentence died on his lips as George discovered that the woman at the table was not Sibby, as the dim light had led him to believe, but a stranger.

"Hello, George," Paul said weakly, equally discomfited. "Uh—how are you?"

George interpreted confusion as guilt. For once glibness deserted him. "Okay, I guess," he mumbled. "Excuse me

—didn't mean to butt in . . ." He backed away, bumping into another table, then fled toward the bar.

"Friend of yours?" Barnes asked.

"Yes. At least, he used to be. He was Sibby's friend before he was mine. I wonder what he's thinking now."

"The worst, of course. People generally do, given the least excuse. Even our best friends. I'm no exception. I'll admit to harboring a few uncharitable thoughts about you myself, Eddie."

Paul felt a tingle of dread. "What do you mean by that?"

"To be blunt about it, I'm wondering if you may be intending to sell me out to Chalk."

The tingle became an aching throb. He managed to reply lightly, "Talk sense, Bob. I can understand your not trusting me, but the proof of my good faith is there on the table. Haven't I done everything you asked?"

"The real question is: Have you done even more than I asked? Forgive my suspicions, Eddie, but I fancy myself as an expert on human behavior. I put myself in your place. Here's a man who wishes only to be free to live his own life. Yet he's dragged against his will into a nasty little war. He couldn't care less which side wins, but he's forced to ally himself with one of them, anyway. Which side does this man choose? Obviously, the side that can offer him what he wants, freedom. I came to the reluctant conclusion that it would be Chalk's side, not mine."

His uncanny intuition, the sixth sense which Paul so greatly feared, had led him to the truth. Paul chose to blunt the accusation with good-natured mockery. "You got me. I'm really a double agent, the camera's empty and this whole setup is a trap. Take a look around. Every man in the room is a Division Five operative. And half the women, too."

"I've already looked. None of Chalk's people is here—but they could be downstairs, waiting for you to finger me as I leave."

Again, the truth; however, Paul detected a note of uncertainty, proof that his bluff had raised doubts in the other man. Barnes, though guessing shrewdly, was still guessing. He didn't know. Paul continued the bluff by pretending to push back his chair, saying, "We'd better not keep Chalk waiting any longer," then gave it a new direction by laughing scornfully. "Come off it, Bob. If you really believed that crap, you wouldn't be here."

Barnes laughed also. "Let's say that I didn't believe it enough to stay away. My hypothesis is based solely on instinct, not evidence. I hope my instinct is wrong about you, Eddie. But in case it isn't, I'd better tell you that I've taken out some life insurance. To be more precise, wife insurance." He held up his arm. "I'm surprised that you didn't recognize my wrist watch. You should—you gave it to Sibby on her last birthday. And the necklace, that was an anniversary present, wasn't it?"

Something was constricting his chest, making breathing difficult. When he spoke, he scarcely recognized the strangled sound as his own voice. "Where is she?"

"With friends. As a matter of fact, Sibby doesn't even know she's a hostage yet. She need never know. If you've dealt honestly with me, she'll be back in your arms within a few hours. If you haven't—if the camera is empty or if I'm prevented from delivering it into the proper hands . . . Well, Nylec has his orders and you know what a methodical creature he is."

"Let her go," Paul begged. "Sibby has nothing to do with this."

"Oh, but she does—simply because she's your wife."

"Take me instead. I'll be your hostage."

"Sorry, Eddie. I believe you value her life more than your own. Which makes her the more valuable hostage. Besides, I already have Sibby and I don't have you." Barnes picked up the cigarette lighter, holding it delicately between thumb and forefinger. "Now that you understand the stakes, do you still want me to take this?"

His impulse was to snatch back the lighter and confess all. But Paul realized that admitting his treachery would not necessarily save Sibby's life and certainly it would not save his own. Neither did he dare permit Barnes to walk into the trap. Without knowing where Sibby was held captive, he could not count on rescuing her before the betrayal was discovered. Yet to allow Barnes to escape was to double-cross Chalk and create a second enemy, equally implacable. Once again he was the man in the middle. The difference was that Sibby now shared that killing ground with him.

He could no longer hope to save himself, but perhaps he could save her; he'd settle for that. "Damn right I want you to take it," he snapped with an indignation which demanded all the acting ability he possessed. "Take it and get out of here. But if Nylec even so much as lays a finger on Sibby, God help you!"

It worked; Barnes sighed. "Believe me, I don't enjoy playing this kind of dirty pool with an old comrade. Take it as a mark of respect. You're one of the few men I've ever been afraid of—perhaps because I consider you my equal. And, after all, you did roger me once." He dropped the cigarette lighter into his purse. "Shall we call it even?"

"Not so fast, old comrade. Where do I find Sibby?"

"Wait here. You'll be notified. I'd estimate two hours. I should be safely across the border into Mexico by then." He rose and smoothed down his skirt. "Oh, you'll get my tab, won't you? It seems unfair to stick you with it under the circumstances, but I understand it's customary."

Paul watched him depart, hips swaying. A number of other male heads turned also; he thought dully that Barnes did make a hell of a good-looking woman. The elevator doors closed behind him. He was gone. Chalk, waiting below for the signal, would have to wait in vain. Of course, he wouldn't wait forever. Long before the vital two hours had elapsed, the Division 5 field supervisor would realize that the ambush had failed. When he discovered that Paul had double-crossed him . . . It was foolish to expect Chalk to take defeat philosophically when victory meant so much to him. His furious reaction would be to salvage what he could by swooping down on Muse, Oatis and by attempting to intercept Barnes at the border. Whereupon Sibby, the innocent hostage for her husband's sins, must inevitably die.

It was up to him to find her before that grim chain of events could be set in motion. For that, he needed his freedom. Barnes might walk out of The Date Bureau without being recognized in his feminine disguise. Paul, with no disguise at all, could not hope to do the same. Chalk's attention must somehow be diverted elsewhere, if only for a moment.

He spied George Dickman standing at the bar. Paul joined him there. "Buy you a drink, pal?"

George regarded him coldly. "What happened to your sister—or was she your maiden aunt from Nebraska? Sorry if I queered your setup."

"No harm done. She wasn't really my type, anyway. I like 'em broken in, not broken down." Paul nudged him roguishly. "Since you haven't scored either, why don't we join forces? You know, grab a couple of good lays and orgy it up across the street at the motel?"

George, like most rakes, possessed a strong streak of the puritan, particularly where his friends were concerned. He drew back as if Paul were infected with a loathsome disease. "We've done a lot of kidding over the years, but I sure never suspected you of really being a two-timer. And on such a grand gal as Sibby, too!"

"Hell, a man needs a little variety now and then. What's wrong with that? Hey, bartender—another drink for my buddy. On me."

"Save your money," George growled. "I'm getting out of here."

He stalked toward the exit, shoulders hunched angrily, hands clenched into fists. He bumped into the maitre d' at the doorway and Paul thought for a moment that George was going to hit the younger man. He took out his anger on the elevator instead, punching the demand button repeatedly until the doors finally parted.

Paul put the tiny walkie-talkie against his mouth. "Barnes is on his way out," he said quietly. "The main elevator. Scrub the previous description. Look for a brown-haired man in a navy blue blazer with a white ascot."

"Roger!" Chalk's voice snapped.

"Who you talking to?" the bartender asked curiously.

"Myself," Paul told him. "I'm a split personality, see? I asked Me if it's time to go home. And Me answered that it sure as hell is. Both of us wish you a pleasant good evening."

He left the bartender staring after him, crossed the noisy room and took the moving sidewalk to the motel.

Sorry, George, he apologized silently as he drove. It was a dirty trick to cast the other man as the decoy. Chalk would undoubtedly give him a rough few minutes before realizing his mistake. Yet George was the least of his concerns. He had cheated Barnes and he had cheated Chalk. One or the other would surely destroy him for it. Could he find Sibby before time ran out?

With no notion where to look, he began at their home.

He was influenced by more than desperation. Perhaps Barnes had lied. Perhaps he had used the threat for the deed and Sibby was not a hostage at all. When he saw a light in the living room, that faint hope swelled to a fierce exultation. Both hope and exultation perished. The Toyota was not in the garage and though he ran through the house, calling her name, there was no reply.

Despair rendered him dizzy. He reeled into a chair, ready to concede defeat. Without an inkling to where she had been taken . . . Then he said aloud, "But the car's gone!" Its absence argued that Sibby had departed under her own power, rather than under duress. If that were so she must have left a note to explain her absence, a courtesy she never omitted. He found it in plain view beside the telephone, where he should have seen it immediately had he not been looking instead for its author.

*Dearest—if you get in before I do, don't panic. You're not the only one who can work nights, so ha-ha! Love, Me.*

He read it over and over, trying to decipher the cryptic message. Think! he commanded himself angrily; the answer's here. Sibby believed she was going to work—where? Doing what? Put it all together, man! Then he heard the voice of Bob Barnes, the off-hand remark that had meant nothing to him at the time: "Sibby doesn't even know she's a hostage yet." Something clicked in his mind. He seized the telephone.

Hank Keller retired early and his family with him. When he finally answered, his voice was gruff with annoyance. Paul wasted no time in apologies. "Lawrence Shevlin," he said. "Describe him for me, Hank."

"What the hell is this? Did you wake me up to play Twenty Questions?" Hank yawned. "Okay, brother-in-law dear, I'll humor you. Shevlin's about forty or forty-five, average height, nearly bald, got a beard—"

"You're a lifesaver," Paul told him gratefully and hung

up. He wondered why it had taken him so long to make the connection. Sibby's glowing description should have been clue enough. Men with Barnes' magnetism and charm were rare; it was unlikely that there could be two in a community as small as Orchestra Beach. Now that he considered it, IBS was the ideal environment for Barnes, both as an academician and as a KGB agent. It allowed the former to exercise his undoubted talent as a teacher. It allowed the latter to work in close conjunction with the defense-oriented firms on the mesa, to cultivate their executives and to pump their wives.

And, finally, to make one of those wives his unwitting weapon. A phone call had been sufficient to arrange it. *Sibby, this is Larry. We're running a little ESP experiment tonight and I wonder if you're free. Oh, your husband's working late? Splendid—we'll be expecting you.*

"But you're not expecting me," Paul said aloud. "That's where your goddam ESP just broke down, Larry."

He had passed the Institute for the Study of the Behavioral Sciences every day for the past two weeks on his way to and from Keller Corp without giving it more than a glance. It had held no special interest for him; tonight it was suddenly the most important spot in the world. Nothing guaranteed that he would find Sibby there, yet when he saw the yellow Toyota in the parking lot he felt no surprise that his assumption was correct.

Paul left his own automobile on the road and approached the starfish-shaped building stealthily on foot. Lights glowed in several of the lower-floor windows. Some stood open to admit the night breeze. But ornamental grillework prevented his entry and though there were at least a half-dozen doors, each was securely locked.

He studied the building for a less conventional entrance. And found it on the upper floor, not actually a floor but a penthouse apparently used for living quarters, surrounded by an immense sun deck. The penthouse was dark. However, the sliding glass door was invitingly ajar, its screen the only barrier. A stout trellis festooned with bougainvillea leaned against one stucco wall. Was it stout enough to bear his weight? It was; he reached the sun deck with relative ease, although his hands bled from encounters with the thorns he could not avoid in the darkness.

The screen was locked. Paul slit it with a key, freed the catch and stepped inside. He stood for a moment, listening, while his eyes grew accustomed to the greater darkness. Satisfied that his entry had triggered no alarms, he removed his shoes and, moving noiselessly, searched the penthouse. It was empty. Sibby's place of captivity was somewhere below.

At the head of the stairs, he hesitated. Somewhere below also was Nylec, and the KGB's disposal man was armed. Paul began a second search of the penthouse, this time for a weapon of his own. Finding none, he settled for a slender statuette with a weighted base. It felt familiar; he realized wryly that it was the figurine of the legendary Tihoya, the Fiesta souvenir for which he himself had posed. He yearned for something more lethal, but this was appropriate, at least.

The stairway terminated in the lobby, the center of the starfish. Corridors branched off like tentacles in five separate directions. All were lighted; all were empty. One presumably led to Sibby—but which? He could not play one-potato-two-potato. He must be right the first time. The PBX board beside the receptionist's desk caught his eye. One key leaned at a different angle from its fellows, indicating a line left open for the use of those remaining in the building. Naturally, Paul thought, Nylec is expecting Barnes to phone him the good news. The key was number 9. Did that refer to an extension or a room? A typewritten directory on the desk supplied the answer: Executive Director, 9.

A glance was sufficient to identify the proper corridor. Shevlin's office lay at the far end, yet when Paul reached it he was presented with a new dilemma. Number 9 was not one room but a suite of three, each with its own door. One was dark, eliminating it as a possibility, but two still remained. While he hesitated, wondering which to storm, a voice cried out his name. "Paul!" For an instant he stood paralyzed by equal parts of surprise and fright. Then he realized that it was Sibby's voice and it had come from behind the door he faced. He plunged into the room, Tihoya held aloft to strike before the assassin might draw his pistol.

The blow was never struck; Nylec was not present. The person who whirled around with an incredulous gasp was Alice, his "wife" from Middletown. She wore a white laboratory smock and her face above it was nearly the same color. "Eddie!" she whispered. "What are you doing here?"

Paul closed the door behind him. "I came for my wife." She lay on a chaise longue beneath a large map of the world. Sibby's eyes were closed as though asleep. Her lips moved and from them came a mumble in which only his name was distinguishable. Yet it was not a greeting; she was unaware of her husband's presence. He thrust Alice aside. "Sibby! Honey, I'm here!" She did not reply and her hand, when he grasped it, exerted no welcoming pressure. Rage rose in him. He swung around to face the other woman. "What in God's name have you done to her?"

Alice had recovered a measure of her composure. "She's just drugged. Pentathol or something like it. I'm not sure —I was told to watch over her."

"Where's Nylec?"

"Napping next door, I think. We didn't expect . . . Bob was right, wasn't he? He suspected you'd gone over to the other side."

"I'm not on any side. That's my crime. All I ever wanted was to be everybody's friend—and instead I wind up everybody's enemy. Are you my enemy too, Alice?"

She looked away. "I should be. But I'm not."

"Then prove it," Paul begged. "Help me get Sibby out of here. I'm not asking for my self. I guess I'm dead already. But Sibby isn't! She shouldn't be made to pay for my crime. Look at her, Alice—that could be you lying there if things had only been different."

"If things had only been different," she repeated in a forlorn voice. "You'll never know how many times I've said that to myself. Or how long I clung to the hope that somehow, someday, you and I . . . That was *my* crime, Eddie." Her eyes searched his face. "But you never really loved me the way you love her, did you?"

Expediency demanded a lie, but he was sick of lying. "No," he said. "I could have, I guess, but I didn't know how to love. When I finally learned, it was too late. Will you help me, anyway?"

She put out a hand and touched his cheek tenderly, a gesture which expressed forgiveness far better than words. "Tell me what you want me to do."

"Take a walk. Go to the ladies' room. Give me five minutes and then start screaming. Bob never has to know that you had anything to do with helping me. He'll think I did it all alone."

"He'll know," she disputed softly. "But I don't care. I'm

already dead, too. I have been for years—ever since Middletown." Her hands found his, closed on them fiercely. "Good-by, Eddie." She turned swiftly toward the door.

It flew open before she could reach it. Nylec was standing there, a long-barreled pistol in his hand, his cold gaze seeking its target. Paul tensed to spring while knowing it was futile. A half-dozen paces separated them, and Nylec was deadly at ten times that distance. Yet though his reaction was nearly instantaneous, Alice's reaction was even faster.

"Thank God!" she cried. "I've been stalling him, hoping you'd—"

"Get out of my way!" Nylec ordered in a voice rendered high-pitched by excitement. The pistol barrel rose while with his other arm he attempted to push the woman out of the line of fire.

Alice grabbed for the weapon with both hands. She was too late to prevent the shot, but not too late to deflect the aim. Paul, leaping forward, felt a paralyzing blow strike his chest. The small caliber bullet staggered him but did not put him down as a .45 would have done. As he strove to regain his balance, there was a second shot. This one was not meant for him, however, but for Alice. Unable to wrest the pistol away from the assassin, she had covered its muzzle with her body. Before there could be a third shot, Paul swung the bronze statuette with all his strength. Nylec's mouth flew open. For a moment he and the woman remained locked together like partners in a macabre dance, then slowly sagged toward the carpet.

Paul pounced on the pistol. There was no further use for it. Tihoya had been weapon enough. Nylec's head lolled at an unnatural angle; the savage blow had broken his neck. Paul turned Alice over gently. Yet this action too was wasted. She had given her life to save his and he would have liked to thank her for it, but all he could do was to stroke her hair and murmur "Hushabye, baby," the phrase they had used to express endearment, so many years ago. He moved her apart from Nylec. It seemed obscene to him somehow that the disposal man and his final victim should embrace each other even in death.

When he rose, the room reeled and he realized that he was mistaken. He, not Alice, was Nylec's final victim. His shirt was wet and the wetness was crimson. His life was ebbing away with his blood; while either remained, he must get Sibby to safety. He tried to lift her from the chaise longue but his strength was unequal to the task. He was able to lift the telephone receiver—and to make the operator understand that she must notify the sheriff.

That done, he sank down on the floor beside his wife. His eyes wanted to close, but he willed them to remain open as he willed his hand to clasp the pistol. After an eternity—it might have been five minutes, or fifty—he heard the wail of a rapidly approaching siren, the screech of tires as a vehicle turned into the parking lot at high speed.

His vision was blurring. He cleared it with an immense effort. "One last look," he muttered. At the two women, one dead and one alive and both for the same reason, that they had loved him. At the KGB pistol, symbol of one life, and at the figurine of Tihoya, symbol of another. And, finally, at the map of the world which bound together Moscow and Prichard, Middletown and Orchestra Beach. It all began to jumble in his mind . . . until he was no longer sure who was dying here tonight, Paul Towers or Eddie Young or Pyotr Avanasov.

# NEITHER

## 3 DIE IN "THINK TANK" SHOOTOUT
### Gunman, 2 Victims
### Perish; Wife Saved

Three persons are dead following a gun battle late last night at the Institute for the Study of the Behavioral Sciences, defense-related "think tank" in Orchestra Beach. Dead are: Paul Towers, electronics firm executive; Mrs. Alice Urich, an employee of the Institute; and an unidentified man believed to be their slayer. A fourth person, Mrs. Sybil Towers, wife of one of the victims, escaped unharmed.

Sheriff's officers believe that the gunman, presumably a burglar, broke into the Institute where the two women were conducting an experiment in extrasensory perception and was surprised there by the arrival of Towers to pick up his wife. In the ensuing struggle, Towers and Mrs. Urich were shot but succeeded in fatally wounding their assailant who died of massive head injuries. Mrs. Towers was treated at Peterson Memorial Hospital and released.

Sheriff's officers are investigating the possibility that the pistol used in the double murder, a .22 caliber automatic of Czech origin, is the same weapon which struck down Fred Rossi in Orchestra Beach last month. Rossi's death is still unsolved.

Staff members of the Institute, which was founded to promote better human relationships, expressed shock at the tragedy. Dr. Lawrence Shevlin, IBS executive director, is currently vacationing in Mexico and could not be reached for comment. . . .

The drive back from the cemetery in the mortuary limousine was silent and somber. When they reached the house on Cabrillo Court, Hank Keller asked his sister if she was sure she wouldn't like them to stay with her for a while. Sibby told him yes, she was quite sure; she was all right now.

Marilyn was still unconvinced. "Come on home with us, at least for a few days," she urged. "I don't like the thought of your being all alone."

"I don't like it much, either," Sibby admitted. "But I guess I'd better start getting used to it."

She watched the limousine drive away before she let herself into the house. "Anybody here?" she called softly.

"In the kitchen," Chalk's voice replied. He and Miss Queen were sitting at the breakfast bar. "Hope you don't mind that we helped ourselves to your coffee. Care for a cup?"

"Please." Watching him pour, she mused, "Funny, I never used to drink much coffee. The last few days that's all I've lived on."

"I know." Miss Queen patted her hand sympathetically. "It's been rough."

Chalk cleared his throat. "How were the services?"

"It was a beautiful funeral—if you can call any funeral

beautiful. The music was lovely and there were so many flowers . . ."

Chalk smiled thinly. "Then I guess the bum got a better sendoff than he deserved."

"He?" Sibby looked startled. "You mean there actually was a body in Paul's coffin? I assumed that—"

"That I'd fill it up with old beer cans? Not when I had a corpse available. It was Fred Rossi, of course. He died in your husband's place. Now he's been buried in his place. Damn appropriate, I'd say."

"I still don't understand it. I mean, why everybody has to believe Paul's dead when he's not and why I can't see him—" She gazed at Chalk with sudden apprehension. "Paul is all right, isnt he? You're not just saying that so—"

"Your husband's alive. It'll take him a while to get over his wound, but he's off the critical list."

"Where is he? You can tell me that much, at least."

"No, I can't, Mrs. Towers. If I did, you wouldn't be able to stay away from him. Now don't look at me like that—you know you wouldn't." He turned to Miss Queen uncomfortably. "Nora, you convince her that this is the way it has to be."

"It's your baby," Miss Queen replied, her sympathy plainly on the side of the other woman. "Convince her yourself."

"Okay," Chalk sighed. "I thought I spelled it out pretty plain the other night at the hospital, but maybe you weren't in any shape to absorb it. Your husband and I made a deal, Mrs. Towers. I agreed to save his life. He agreed to help me catch Bob Barnes, the man you knew as Shevlin. Well, I kept my part of the bargain. Your husband didn't keep his."

"You know why he didn't. Because of me."

"The fact remains that he let Barnes, maybe the top Soviet agent in the United States, get away. So maybe you don't think that matters a hell of a lot. I think different. A man like Barnes is worth a couple of divisions to the other side. I'll admit that when I found your husband out there at IBS I was mad enough to shoot him myself. Then I realized I'd be better off keeping him alive if I could."

"Joe's all heart," Miss Queen observed dryly.

"Knock it off, Nora," Chalk growled. "I'm telling it like it is. I had to salvage what I could from the fiasco. It was too late to grab Barnes. He was across the Mexican border by then on the way back to Russia with the secret plans for SWORD in his pocket."

"The phony secret plans," Miss Queen amended.

"Sure, they're phonies, but Barnes doesn't know that. I figure that if I can keep him believing they're the genuine article, the Soviet scientists will waste six months, maybe even longer, trying to make the contraption work before they find out they've been had. That's six months we'll have to get SWORD operational—and six months we won't have to worry about the KGB trying to steal it because they'll think they already have."

Sibby, who had been following the explanation intently, frowned. "You still haven't answered my question. What reason is there to pretend that Paul's dead? Your scheme would work just as well without that."

"That's only half of the scheme. If the KGB knew that Paul Towers is alive, they'd assume that he would blow the whistle on their whole apparatus—IBS, Muse, Oatis, clear back to that publishing company in Chicago. He'd have no reason not to. They'd simply do a gopher and set up new covers. I'd rather they stay in business at the same old stand. That way we can keep them under surveillance, maybe even infiltrate their organization. But even more important, at least to me personally, is that Bob Barnes will be coming back to this country sooner or later, probably sooner. Not as Lawrence Shevlin, naturally—I expect to hear any day that Dr. Shevlin has met with an unfortunate accident down in Mexico—but as somebody. Paul is the one man who can positively identify him. He's the one man Barnes is afraid of, because they think alike. So I'm going to use him like a Geiger counter until someday he goes click—click—click . . ."

Sibby asked faintly, "Has Paul agreed to be your—your Geiger counter?"

"I didn't give him a choice."

"But if I refuse to go along with—"

"I'm not giving you a choice, either. Right now only the four of us know the truth—five if you count the doctor who signed the death certificate, and he works for me. That's the way it's got to stay." Chalk regarded her bleakly. "You think I'm a grade-A monster, right? Okay, let me ask you a question. If you were to bring Paul back to life, how long do you suppose Barnes would let him stay that way, fearing him like he does?"

"Couldn't you protect him?"

"Not here. Not as Paul Towers. Since he's got to go underground anyway, why not make it look like he's six feet underground? Believe me, it's the best way for all of us—including Paul."

There was a silence and then Sibby sighed. "I guess you're right. I don't really have a choice. Well, we'll just have to make the best of it, that's all. When can I see Paul?"

"I can't say exactly. If all goes well, I'll arrange a meeting—maybe in a year or so."

"A year or so! You can't be serious!"

"Eddie Young fooled the KGB into thinking him dead. They're naturally going to wonder if Paul Towers hasn't pulled the same trick. As a matter of fact, one of their agents dropped by the mortuary trying to get them to open the closed coffin. So I expect they'll be watching you, Mrs. Towers. That's the reason Nora and I sneaked in here today by the back door."

"But a whole year!" Sibby quavered, tears welling in her eyes.

Miss Queen put a consoling arm around her shoulders. "A year isn't forever, honey. If Paul was in the service, he'd be gone longer than that. Keep busy and the time will pass faster than you think."

"Nora's right," Chalk agreed heartily. "And later on, when the situation warrants, you can tell everybody you've got a job in some other part of the country to explain your moving away—" He stopped, puzzled at her fresh expression of dismay. "I thought you understood that. Paul Towers is dead and buried. He can never come back to Orchestra Beach."

"Shut up, Joe," Miss Queen advised through clenched teeth. "Hasn't she had enough for one day?"

"It's all right." Sibby brushed away her tears and managed a tremulous smile. "I'm a big girl now. I don't care what it costs or how long it takes. I'll wait for Paul."

"How about a late lunch—or an early supper?" Chalk suggested as they drove back into the center of town. "I'm starved."

"I'm not," Miss Queen said. "I feel a little sick to my stomach. That brave kid! Did you have to be so rough on her?"

"I'm not rough. Life is. She's going to need to face the fact eventually that there's never going to be any completely happy ending."

"You don't think she means what she says about waiting for him? I do."

"Sure, she means it now. But a year is a long time. She'll have plenty of lonely hours to brood about it . . . and for understanding what she's in for. She'll be saying good-by to a hell of a lot, Nora—home, friends, maybe even her family. What does she get in exchange? Not security, certainly. Towers will never be really safe, no matter where he goes or what new identity he takes. There's always the chance that somebody from the past will recognize him. That next time the bullets won't hit the wrong man. They'll never be able to make any real friends. If they have a child—and you know she wants one badly— she'll be scared every minute of what might happen to it. I'd say it adds up to a pretty big price to pay for a man who, to be blunt about it, has lied to her from the first day they met."

"You're forgetting one thing. She loves him."

"I don't know much about love. I do know something about human nature. Sibby's a damn attractive woman. There'll be a lot of men courting the young widow, men with no built-in problems. Not to mention that the longer she lives without Paul, the easier it'll get."

Miss Queen eyed him skeptically. "Be honest, Joe. Is that what you really think will happen—or what you secretly want to happen? You haven't forgiven Paul for crossing you."

"I'm not as big a bastard as everybody seems to think. Deep down, I kind of admire Towers. He told me once that he'd like a world where there'd be no need for men like Barnes and me. Well, I'd like that, too. Matter of fact, I'd like that very much. But it'll never happen."

"Why not?"

"Because we won't let it. Not just people like me but
. . ." He gestured at the busy sidewalks they were passing. "We all look out for number one—and that means to
hell with numbers two through four billion. I'm betting
Sibby's no different. When the time comes for her to make
the big sacrifice, she'll decide that Paul Towers is better
dead, after all."

"I'm betting you're wrong," Miss Queen said stub-
bornly. "About Sibby—and maybe everything else, too."

"You know what? I hope to God I am wrong." Chalk
sighed. "And not just for Sibby's sake. Or Paul's. For all
of us."

# A THRILLING
# SUSPENSE TRILOGY
# by CLIVE EGLETON

"... these Egleton books are among the best of their type."
—*The San Francisco Chronicle*

Russia has devastated Britain with a nuclear attack and is occupying the country. The English people unite against this oppression and form an underground resistance network to fight for their freedom against seemingly overwhelming odds.

## LAST POST FOR A PARTISAN

Five years after the holocaust a split in England's resistance is jeopardizing the entire movement. David Garnett is called in to find and eliminate the traitors in a deadly game of violence and intrigue in which everyone is suspect.

P344     $1.25

## A PIECE OF RESISTANCE

It is the near future and England has been conquered and occupied by the Soviets. When the assassin of a high Russian official is captured and sent to a maximum-security prison, the underground resistance plots an incredible mission to rescue the assassin.

P315     $1.25

## THE JUDAS MANDATE

In the final novel of this electrifying trilogy, David Garnett must carry out his riskiest assignment yet, involving the release of political prisoners who will try to form a government in exile in the United States.

P352     $1.25

# ALL NEW DYNAMITE SERIES

# THE DESTROYER

## by Richard Sapir & Warren Murphy

CURE, the world's most secret crime-fighting organization created the perfect weapon — Remo Williams — man programmed to become a cold, calculating death machine. The super man of the 70's!

**TO ORDER**
Please check the space next to the book/s you want, send this order form together with your check or money order, include the price of the book/s and 25¢ for handling and mailing, to:
PINNACLE BOOKS, INC. / P.O. Box 4347
Grand Central Station / New York, N.Y. 10017
☐ Check here if you want a free catalog.
I have enclosed $_____ check_____ or money order_____
as payment in full. No C.O.D.'s.
Name_____
Address_____
City_____ State_____ Zip_____
(Please allow time for delivery.)